Critical Acclaim for *English Lessons and Other Stories*

1996 Friends of American Writers Award

"Each of these superb short stories shuttles between the intricate threads of family, the rich sturdy fabric of ancient Indian tradition, and the somewhat more ready-to-wear culture of North America."
— *The Georgia Straight*

"Positions and postures are finely drawn . . . . Every detail is for a purpose. . . . Always present is a lively, active, questioning spirit."
— *Books in Canada*

"Baldwin presents a kaleidoscope of issues: the clash of cultures, sexual, social, racial and religious chauvinism, ancient enmities, generational misunderstandings, the stressful adjustments of immigrants."
— *The Chronicle Herald*

"*English Lessons and Other Stories* chronicles the vicious circle of Indian women attempting to balance traditional roles with views and lifestyles outside their inherited gender and homeland."
— *The National Post*

"Singh Baldwin writes with a restrained passion which describes the friction between East and West, traditional and modern."
— *The Asian Age*

"A writer from an ethnic minority who writes frankly about his or her community takes enormous risks. It is to Shauna Singh Baldwin's credit that she had been unafraid to step on a few toes . . . Baldwin's prose is precise, nuanced and sensual. She threads her stories with ravishing glints of colour that explode against the pallid landscape of Canad~ ") *Star*

Other fiction by SHAUNA SINGH BALDWIN

We Are Not in Pakistan (2007)
What the Body Remembers (2004)
The Tiger Claw (1999)
A Foreign Visitor's Survival Guide to America (Co-author, 1992)

ENGLISH LESSONS AND OTHER STORIES

Shauna Singh Baldwin

Rupa & Co

Typeset by
Mindways Design
1410 Chiranjiv Tower
43 Nehru Place
New Delhi 110 019

Printed in India by
Nutech Photolithographers
B-240, Okhla Industrial Area, Phase-I,
New Delhi 110 020, India

1006666835

Look not at my finger,
Look where I am pointing
— author unknown

Contents

Contents

Acknowledgements

This book began from *Sunno! (Listen)*, "the East-Indian American Radio Show where you don't have to be Indian to listen," an audio magazine I produced and hosted for three years on WYMS in Milwaukee. My thanks to listeners who called and asked me to write more stories to be read on air. Among the many people who helped me with this book, my special thanks go to Dr. Marilyn M. Levine, Pegi Taylor, and my husband David Baldwin, for many hours of philosophical discussion about these stories.

My late grandfather, Sardar Bahadur Sarup Singh, was the oral storyteller behind "Rawalpindi 1919," which first appeared in *Rosebud* magazine. My parents' experience in Canada was inspiration for "Montreal 1962," and I thank the editors of *Hum* and *Fireweed*, where it first appeared. For their Punjabi maxims, translated and included in these stories, I thank the real Ma Dropadi, and Atma Singh. For research assistance in India, I am indebted to Ena Singh. For research assistance and hospitality in Canada, my thanks to Satinder and Bea Singh. For their encouragement, I thank writers Anjana Appachana, Bapsi Sidhwa, Robert Olen Butler and Chris Loken. Many thanks to Madhu Kishwar and her staff at *Manushi Magazine: A Journal about Women and Society in India*, where "English Lessons," "A Pair of Ears," and

"Simran" first appeared in print; to the editors of *Cream City Review*, who nominated "Family Ties" for a Pushcart Prize; and to *Calyx*, where "Jassie" was first published. After winning the 1995 Writers' Union of Canada Short Prose Competition for Developing Writers, "Jassie" also appeared in *Books in Canada*. For their faith in me, I am always grateful to the late Bibiji Sukhwant Kaur, Sardar Kishen Singh and Sardarni Raminder Sarup Singh. For her exact editing, my grateful appreciation to Laurel Boone at Goose Lane Editions.

Shauna Singh Baldwin
Milwaukee

Rawalpindi 1919

Whole wheat flour and water. Not just any flour will do either, she thought. He is very particular about that. Choudhary Amir Singh would dine on simple fare, but the first chapatti must be made from the wheat of his own mills and it must come from the hands of the mother of his sons — Sardarni Sahib herself.

It seems warmer than usual, she thought, as her fingers moulded and formed the dough, knuckling into it, brown soft hands suppling it, readying it as she had made her sons ready. And for what, she thought. The elder a poet. Gentle and kind but no businessman. What would he make of the flour mill? Now the younger one, he's more worldly. Twenty-one years old and Choudhary Sahib had found no bride worthy of him — yet.

She made a ball of the dough . . . patting . . . patting . . . smoothing the wet, glistening gold-flecked ball. Now dig a small ball out of the large one. Cut it apart from the whole. Now shape it, roll it between the palms. She looked at the small ball cradled in her hand. At this stage, she could still return it to the large ball and no damage would be apparent. She could knead it back and it would blend again.

But this idea, who knows where it came from. This idea that her boy could go to Vilayat, to the white people's country, to learn from their gurus in their dark and cloudy cities — her youngest — and then return to Rawalpindi, and his people would know no difference. She shook her head. Hai toba!

It will be different in three years, she thought. Today Choudhary Amir Singh washes his hands after shake-hand with an Angrez, the collector with the brown topi and the red face. But Sarup is a friendly boy and he will have Angrez boys as friends and he will learn the shake-hand instead of our no-polluting palms-together Sat Sri Akal.

A little flour on the ball now. Just a dusting. Enough to swirl the ball between her thumbs and the first two fingers of her hands. Round and round, faster and faster, flatter and flatter, larger and larger, thinner and thinner.

He would look thinner after three years. She tried to imagine him. They would expect him to tie his beard, his long dark beard, up under his chin. She would be sure he had enough turbans to last two months on the boat and three years in Inglaand. Some silk ones — oh, the brightest colours — so the Angrez would know he came from a bold Sikh clan. But he would be thinner, with no woman to cook chapattis. Sardar Baldev Singh had been to London, and he had told her he had eaten only boiled food with not a single chilli all the time. Perhaps he said it as an excuse for his appetite on his return, but she'd noticed even quite high-up Angrez were thin. It must be their food. Sarup would never become used to that.

She rolled the chapatti with a rolling pin, picked it up and deftly slapped it from one palm to the other. Then whoosh — onto the tava over the coal fire. She steadied the tava with one hand, and, with a small rag in the other hand, rotated the chapatti till it was almost cooked.

But perhaps there were other customs he would get used to. He had already, she knew, bought an English book to read, now it was agreed he would be studying in Vilayat. She had seen it and it had an Englishwoman and a man in a black English suit on the outside. They were kissing, but Sarup told her it was a classic, like the story of Roop-Basant. He said all the English stories like "Roop-Basant" are written down, and in Imperial College, there were even people whose only study was to learn those stories. This one was called *Thelma,* he said. It was written by a woman called Marri Corrilli. Now how could this be, that a woman would write such a fat book. But maybe she was a poor woman who could not afford to get a munshi to write down her thoughts.

She took the chapatti off the tava. Quick, snatch the tava off the fire and replace it with the chapatti. She watched as the chapatti rose into a hot-air-filled dough balloon. Just at its peak she lifted it from the fire and set it on the ground on a steel thali to cool.

It was the thali that brought it to mind. Angrez don't use steel thalis. They use white plates. They don't use the chapatti, breaking off a small piece to scoop up their food. They use sharp forks and long knives — straight ones, not curved like our kirpans — to keep themselves distant from their food. He will have to learn that.

And as she rose from her haunches to pick up the thali and covered her head with her chunni in preparation for entering her husband's presence, she decided to talk with him about it. She moved to the doorway and stepped over the wooden threshold.

"Ay, Ji," she said. She would not bring him misfortune by using his name.

Choudhary Amir Singh looked up from the divan and cushions on the floor.

"You will need to buy chairs for this house when he returns," she said. "And we will need plates."

Montreal 1962

In the dark at night you came close and your voice was a whisper though there is no one here to wake. "They said I could have the job if I take off my turban and cut my hair short." You did not have to say it. I saw it in your face as you took off your new coat and galoshes. I heard their voices in my head as I looked at the small white envelopes I have left in the drawer, each full of one more day's precious dollars — the last of your savings and my dowry. Mentally, I converted dollars to rupees and thought how many people in India each envelope could feed for a month.

This was not how they described emigrating to Canada. I still remember them saying to you, "You're a well-qualified man. We need professional people." And they talked about freedom and opportunity for those lucky enough to already speak English. No one said then, "You must be reborn white-skinned — and clean-shaven to show it — to survive." Just a few months ago, they called us exotic new Canadians, new blood to build a new country.

Today I took one of my wedding saris to the neighbourhood dry-cleaner and a woman with no eyebrows held it like a dishrag as she asked me, "Is it a bed sheet?"

"No," I said.

"Curtains?"

"No."

I took the silk back to our basement apartment, tied my hair in a tight bun, washed the heavy folds in the metal bathtub, and hung it, gold threads glinting, on a drip-dry hanger.

When I had finished, I spread a bed sheet on the floor of the bathroom, filled my arms with the turbans you'd worn last week and knelt there surrounded by the empty soft hollows of scarlet, navy, earth brown, copper, saffron, mauve and bright parrot green. As I waited for the bathtub to fill with warm soapy water, I unravelled each turban, each precise spiral you had wound round your head, and soon the room was full of soft streams of muslin that had protected your long black hair.

I placed each turban in turn on the bubbly surface and watched them grow dark and heavy, sinking slowly, softly into the warmth. When there were no more left beside me, I leaned close and reached in, working each one in a rhythm bone-deep, as my mother and hers must have done before me, that their men might face the world proud. I drained the tub and new colours swelled — deep red, dark black mud, rust, orange, soft purple and jade green.

I filled the enamel sink with clean water and starch and lifted them as someday I will lift children. When the milky bowl had fed them, my hands massaged them free of alien red-blue water. I placed them carefully in a basin and took them out into our grey two rooms to dry.

I placed a chair by the window and climbed on it to tie the four corners of each turban length to the heavy curtain rod. Each one in turn, I drew out three yards till it was folded completely in two. I grasped it firmly at its sides and swung my hands inward. The turban furrowed before me. I arced my hands outward and it became a canopy. Again inward, again outward, hands close, hands apart, as though I was back in Delhi on a flat roof under a hot sun or perhaps near a green field of wheat stretching far to the banks of the Beas.

As the water left the turbans, I began to see the room through muslin screens. The pallid walls, the radiator you try every day to turn up hotter for me, the small windows, unnaturally high. When the turbans were lighter, I set the dining chairs with their halfmoon backs in a row in the middle of the well-worn carpet and I draped the turbans over their tops the way Gidda dancers wear their chunnis pinned tight in the centre parting of their hair. Then I sat on the carpet before them, willing them: dance for me — dance for us. The chairs stood as stiff and wooden as ignorant Canadians, though I know maple is softer than chinar.

Soon the bands of cloth regained all their colour, filling the room with sheer lightness. Their splendour arched upwards, insisting upon notice, refusing the drabness, refusing obscurity, wielding the curtain rod like the strut of a defending champion.

From the windows over my head came the sounds of a Montreal afternoon, and the sure step of purposeful feet on the sidewalk. Somewhere on a street named in English where the workers speak joual I imagined your turban making its way in the crowds, bringing you home to me.

Once again I climbed on a chair and I let your turbans loose. One by one, I held them to me, folding in their defiance, hushing their unruly indignation, gentling them into temporary submission. Finally, I faced them as they sat before me.

Then I chose my favourite, the red one you wear less and less, and I took it to the bedroom. I unfurled the gauzy scarlet on our bed and it seemed as though I'd poured a pool of the sainted blood of all the Sikh martyrs there. So I took a corner and tied it to the doorknob just as you do in the mornings instead of waking me to help you. I took the diagonal corner to the very far end of the room just as you do, and rolled the scarlet inward as best I could within the cramped four walls. I had to untie it from the doorknob again to roll the other half, as I used to every day for my father, then my brother and now you. Soon the scarlet rope lay ready.

I placed it before the mirror and began to tie it as a Sardar would, one end clenched between my teeth to anchor it, arms raised to sweep it up to the forehead down to the nape of the neck, around again, this time higher. I wound it swiftly, deftly, till it jutted haughtily forward, adding four inches to my stature. Only when I had pinned the free end to the peak did I let the end clenched between my teeth fall. I took the saliva-darkened cord, pulled it back where my hair bun rested low, and tucked it up over the turban, just as you do.

In the mirror I saw my father as he must have looked as a boy, my teenage brother as I remember him, you as you face Canada, myself as I need to be.

The face beneath the jaunty turban began to smile.

I raised my hands to my turban's roundness, eased it from my head and brought it before me, setting it down lightly before the mirror. It asked nothing now but that I be worthy of it.

And so, my love, I will not let you cut your strong rope of hair and go without a turban into this land of strangers. The knot my father tied between my chunni and your turban is still strong between us, and it shall not fail you now. My hands will tie a turban every day upon your head and work so we can keep it there. One day our children will say, "My father came to this country with very little but his turban and my mother learned to work because no one would hire him."

Then we will have taught Canadians what it takes to wear a turban.

Dropadi Ma

The monsoon rains curtained the windows all afternoon and Dropadi Ma held me on her lap and told me long stories. I knew them all by now and followed her toothless chant with my lips. She never said I was getting too big to sit in her lap — just covered us both in her raggedy shawl, her chocolate hands over my pale ones. Sometimes she would fall silent, thinking, remembering, and in the middle of one story would tell me a small one about the days when my mother or one of her brothers had been small enough to sit in her lap and listen. And then we would return to the story chant, smoothly re-entering webs of treachery, violence and sacrifice upon sacrifice, every story set in an age of obedience where the only conflicts lay between duty and duty. Stories to keep a child from wandering too far.

And yet my mother's brothers had all wandered far. Sukhimama, the uncle I knew least of all, lived in Montreal, where there is no monsoon, and had returned to be married to someone my grandfather had decreed acceptable. My parents and I would fly to Bangkok for the wedding.

Dropadi Ma wanted to be there too, I felt it, for Sukhimama was the eldest boy, the one she had taught most. But Dropadi

Ma was, at the end of it all, only a servant, and we all knew the question would not arise. So instead she oversaw every detail of the packing, holding his wedding uchkan close to her face so she could see that every gold button was threaded with gold thread, not lemon-coloured, and placing one of her own gold bangles with the jewellery our family was to give to the bride's family.

But even in the few days since Sukhimama had returned, we both felt there was more than monsoon pressure in the house. My grandfather's roar was louder, and he would come to the long dinner table at the gong and would correct my table manners all through dinner, over my mother's gentle protests. I hid in closets a lot, just to read, and heard Sukhimama talking to my grandfather.

"I tell you, she may be a very nice girl, but I do not know her. It is not 1945 anymore, Darji, it is 1966."

My grandfather's voice came low like the growl of a tiger reaching the end of its patience. "What will come of knowing her, may I ask? And if, after this 'knowing her,' you think you do not want her, what will we do then? By then her reputation will be ruined and I will have to pay her parents to find a lesser match. Did they addle your brain in Canada? You should have stayed in England, sir. The English understand these things."

I was all ready to run for refuge from the wrath that would follow any reply to so logical an argument, but I heard Sukhimama sigh and I knew the storm was averted. Dropadi Ma would be glad.

But when I told her, I could not tell if she was glad. She fell silent for a long time, so I entered into the silence with her and we thought our separate thoughts together, cross-legged on the kitchen floor. She took a few handfuls of dal seeds and began to pick them over on a metal tray, looking for tiny stones that could grit in our mouths. Her eyes were right close to the tray and it took her a long time to find a few. I began to believe she had moved on to thinking about other things. But then her leathery brown face with the big mole on the nose came around to mine and her eyes behind her Coke-bottle glasses looked into mine, and she pointed to her wrist and said, "Go. Bring my bangle back to me."

My heart started to pound. "Maji, what if I am caught?"

"You will tell them you were obeying Dropadi Ma. Have I no rights in this house? It is my bangle, and I would have it back. Go and reclaim it for me, but quietly."

I walked out of the cool dark kitchen into rooms of covered furniture and trunks half-filled for the month-long celebration in Bangkok. I had seen my grandmother place the bangle in the big silver-coloured trunk. Two minutes of breath-held scrabbling inside and it was in my hand. I fled back to Dropadi Ma. Her hand closed over it, but she did not place it back on her wrist. Instead, she lifted her chunni and slipped it between her comfortable breasts.

"Tell Sukhiji I would like to speak with him when he can find the time." It was a command.

"Dropadi Ma meant right now, Uncle. When she says, 'When You Can Find The Time,' she means, 'Now, If You Love Me,' Uncle. Come quick. Maybe she is sick — she never commands us."

He came quickly, filling the doorway of the kitchen where she sat with her head covered, his big hands folded and his turbaned head dropped to ask her blessing. I wondered if they ask a blessing from their elders in Canada, for he had not forgotten how. His laugh boomed in the small kitchen as he crouched to give her a hug and then sat on the floor next to us. "Yes, Maji?" There was a little Canadian accent in his Yes, I thought. I pretended to be invisible; they thought I was too small to understand.

Soon the gold bangle appeared and passed from her hands to his two cupped hands. Her right hand rested briefly on his shoulder and I heard her say, "Jeeo, Beta." Live, my son. And then, "Khushi Raho." May you be happy.

A few days later, when all the trunks were locked and marigold garlands of farewell lay ready for preflight ceremonies in the rose-grey dawn, there was a shout and then a woman, my grandmother maybe, cried out, "We are ruined!"

He was gone. A 2:00 a.m. Air Canada flight, I heard. Direct to Montreal. Then an argument. You can't fly direct to Montreal. Perhaps Air Canada will stop in London and we can call a relative to talk to him there. Who has a relative there? Call him, call him! Tell him to talk to Sukhi at the airport. Remind him of his duty. Tell him how much money we will have to pay the girl's family. Hai, book a call to Bangkok, to the girl's father! They will be expecting us on the plane, today. We are ruined.

I ran to find Dropadi Ma, barefoot as I was. But she was not in the servant's quarter on her charpai as usual. She was already on her corner of the kitchen floor, and she was wearing yesterday's clothes. Her glasses lay on the floor beside her and she held one knee as she dozed. I shook her a little.

"Dropadi Ma — Sukhimama has taken a flight to Canada last night. There can be no wedding!"

Her toothless smile was wide and joyous. "Come, little one. Ma will tell you a story."

Family Ties

Everyone says Inder is the smart one and I the steady one. I know steady means boring but it doesn't matter; he's my brother. He's the thin one, and I'm the one Mummy calls Fatty. He's the one with laughter and he always asks why. "Why?" is a question Mummy takes as a personal affront, but Inder asks it over and over. Why can't we live in Indore with Dad? Or in Darjeeling with old Bibiji and Nana? Why can't we play Gulli Danda with the big-eyed, bandy-legged jhuggi children? Why doesn't Mummy allow him to sing like Rajesh Khanna in the films — winking at girls, with his right hand twirling in time to the music?

I am ten and he is fourteen and he challenges me to play mental chess through the mosquito nets separating our beds, and I hear him whisper "check" by my fifth move. And every night he tells me stories. There is his favourite — the one about the sons of Guru Gobind Singh who were interred alive in a brick wall but who did not convert to Islam. Then there is my favourite — the one about Guru Nanak falling asleep with his feet pointing towards Mecca. I make Inder tell me how the qazis came upon him and tried to move his feet to a more respectful place, and how the Ka'aba spun till Guru Nanak awoke and suggested they try pointing his feet at any place where God is not. Most nights, the chucka-chucka-chuck of the three-armed overhead fan lulls me to sleep and leaves him to finish his stories alone.

When winter comes, Mummy buys a TV from Nancy and Pierre, her Canadian diplomat friends. Inder and I sit on the threadbare oriental carpet, watching clips of old Hindi films and the endless agricultural shows, huddled together with our knees propping up the warm tent of a bulbous silk razzai. I gaze enthralled at the blue-grey glow for the news while Inder imitates the pompous, stilted voices of the announcers trying so hard to sound like the BBC: "THIS is the news. Today the government announced that President Mujib Rehman has asked for the support of the Indian Army's brave jawans in defence of the Muktibahini in Bangladesh." Now the nightly stories have Dad attired as Guru Gobind Singh from two hundred years ago, wearing a saffron turban, wielding a huge kirpan — and leading the 61st Cavalry.

Mummy orders Dad's old driver, Nand Singh, to paint the upper half of the headlights of our Ambassador black, in preparation for blackouts. And Dad comes home the night we hear the first sirens wail their warning.

Dad doesn't wear a saffron turban or carry a big kirpan. He isn't even as large as I remembered, and he looks a little worn. Mummy and he use a servant as their messenger when they need to talk — or me, because I can say the English name of Dad's department in the government as he speculates about his next posting. And all the time Inder asks, "Aren't you going to be in the war?"

"No," Dad replies. "I lost enough in '47."

It's true, I know, because Nand Singh has told me the story of Partition. He has told me how Dad and my Dada and my Dadi locked their haveli near Rawalpindi before the Muslims came and how they fled on a death train and only twenty-one-year-old Dad arrived in the new India because Nand Singh and he used their turbans to rope themselves to the belly of the railcar and hid beneath it with a revolver as their only weapon while Dada and Dadi's screams filled the mad swirling darkness. I know Dad is thinking of his parents when he wanders off to a quiet spot, takes off his shoes, sits cross-legged before the Granth Sahib and says the words of the Gurus, chanting low. I stand behind him keeping the flies away with his special silver-handled yak's-hair tail, white and rough as my Dada's beard might have been, and when he nods I turn the pages of the tome for him.

"Beti." I am absurdly happy when he looks up and his teeth flash white in the dark cloud of his beard.

On television they begin in monotones to tell children how to take shelter in concrete pipes placed along the roadsides. Dad smells my fear and jokes that I am a silly little kukri, a hen instead of a Sikhni of our family of whom he can be proud.

Inder tells me Gnat is a name for a baby fly and also a new Indian aeroplane that Pakistani General Yahya Khan won't be able to get away from. But now a small bomb has fallen on the outskirts of Delhi and the streets are deserted at midday. Even the street vendor who spins white sugar clouds he calls Old Women's Hair doesn't ring his bicycle bell at our gate, although I am home because school is closed for the war. Only the sparrows in our eucalyptus tree are undaunted, so I give them crumbs of the bread that Mummy complains is so expensive.

Nand Singh takes me to the market with him, opening the back seat door for me as though I were Mummy and shooing away the poor jhuggi boys with their oversized empty coolie baskets. Though he cannot read or write, he knows what the ration cards say and he has such a good memory he never forgets even one item Mummy tells him to buy. We pick our way through shady gullies between the jute-bag-roofed shops of corrugated tin, and the disappointed cries of fishmongers follow us to the stall of the chicken-seller.

The chicken-seller sits before a stack of metal cages and his brown belly spills over a blood-flecked once-white dhoti. He spits betelnut juice at a gutter at our feet and offers me a red-gummed smile. Nand Singh points to the hens, four to each tiny cage, and says graciously, "Which one would mem-sahib like?" He's complimenting my judgement in advance, letting me know I have grown up enough to be trusted with some household decisions. The hens all look the same to me — brownish-white with frightened eyes, silly kukris just like me. I look at the closest cage and one steps forward. She holds her head high when she crows, thrusts her breast at the cage and seems unafraid to die, so I say, "That one." A moment later, her head is severed and Nand Singh throws her in his shopping bag. Although Mummy's frown at my plate warns that no one will marry a fatty, I eat the curried kukri that night, hoping her courage will nourish mine.

When Inder says he wants to run away to join the jawans, Dad and Mummy don't even notice. They're fighting again over money. Always money. She says Dad should be like every other government employee — take a favour here, a perk there, a bribe here, have a little consideration for his family. Try to get a Delhi posting — she says it's the only place a government servant can make better money. He says she should not want foreign-made goods; he is working hard so that Indians can make all the things she wants. She says he is making her do without the things he can well afford. I run back and forth with messages until Mummy tells me to tell Dad she agreed to marry him only to save Nana the price of a dowry because Dad had said he didn't want one. I take that message outside and tell it to my sparrows instead. When I go into my father's room, he looks at my frightened face and says to tell her all right, she can buy us an air conditioner and pay Nancy and Pierre three thousand rupees.

When I return, he pats the air with a cupped right hand, so I sink to the floor before him.

"You have a faint heart, beti, a faint heart that can bring dishonour to those who love you. You are becoming just like my sister."

He rises, takes a battered attaché case from his steel almirah, places it carefully beside him and removes a woman's picture. I crane my neck over his knees to see it.

The woman in the picture looks kind though she has no smile. A pale chunni covers her head and her face is fair and round as a winter moon. An artist's brush has retouched the photo so her eyes are gold-flecked brown like mine. I say, "I did not know you had a sister."

Inder stands watching at the door, his legs two long cylinders above the bell-bottoms of the imported blue jeans Mummy just bought from Nancy.

Dad's lips vanish into his beard as he surveys his son's attire, but then he says, "Come in."

We stand before the open case, our unknown aunt looking up at us.

"What was her name?" I ask.

"Whose name?"

"Your sister's. My aunt's."

"Chandini Kaur."

Moonlight Princess. Of course that should be her name.

"How old is she in this picture?"

"She was eighteen in 1947."

But Dad is lifting something else from the attaché case — a triangular muslin bundle. He unwraps it slowly before us until a black thing is exposed. A revolver. Sleek, slender-muzzled. Outside, a siren shrieks and then subsides.

To my brother he says, "Beta, I do not know if you will ever need this. But there is a war now, and I want you to know how to use it to defend this little kukri."

Our faces solemn, we follow him upstairs to the sun-swathed concrete terrace, so high the leaves of our eucalyptus tree are close against the parapet. Our eyes never leave the weapon.

He makes us stand five paces behind him. The bullets clink as he loads them into the chamber. He takes aim and fires.

Leaves and feathers explode from the eucalyptus. I must not cry.

"Now you try." He gives my brother the gun, shows him how to close one eye, take the safety catch off, aim. Fire. When he misses, Dad shrugs, "If you need to use it, you will not miss. Marksmanship is in your blood."

We descend to Dad's room again and help him wrap the weapon away. It is smooth and cool to the touch, as death must be.

Then, with his hand on my head, he tells my brother, "If the Muslims come and your sister is in danger, you must shoot her rather than let her fall into their hands."

My breath comes fast when I hear this, and I feel his hand on my head like the kukri must have felt the chicken-seller's pudgy gentle hand reaching into her cage. I look to my brother.

But my brother looks only at my father and he says, "I will."

I want to shout at them — I am your daughter. I am your sister. But my tongue has turned slow, slow as a monsoon slug I once saw Inder flick from our scrap of garden into the dust of the street. I look at my aunt Chandini's miniature face and then at my father's. The small face of a woman whose name is never mentioned, and the set face of a man who has upheld his family's honour. A plane roars over the house and, for the first time, I feel no rush of fear; far more is the danger from those within. Dad locks the Moonlight Princess away again in his steel almirah.

My brother does not look at me again that day. At night, he

does not whisper heroic tales of the Gurus to send me to sleep but lies on his other side, face averted. We are rice saplings separated for transplanting. I lie on my creaky string bed gazing at the latent vortex of the ceiling fan and wonder if he will have the courage to kill me to defend me, and where will I find the courage to die as Chandini Kaur must have, soft heart offered at eighteen to her brother's bullet? My father's bullet. Is it worse to be caught, converted, killed or raped by Muslims than to be killed by a brother? A brother — my brother — who said "I will" in the voice of his warrior ancestors without once asking his usual everyday everlasting "Why?"

The Moonlight Princess comes to me in my dreams that night, telling me I can trust no one. Especially if he says he loves me.

The twenty-five days of war are long, and when school opens again my new teacher is a Muslim — Miss Shafi, who wears a sleeveless sari blouse and ties her petticoat low below her navel so her midriff swivels through the corridors. She asks us to turn to the map of the subcontinent in our geography books and write "Bangladesh" in place of "East Pakistan."

Now I am eleven. My brother is sent away to a boarding school because Dad says he needs to be taught some more what it means to be a man. He writes me only one letter to tell me he has fought with the Hindu boys who teased him about his turban, and that the Drama Master made him take the woman's part in a school play. I think of him, forced to dress as a woman and paraded before an audience without the turban that would protect his waist-length hair, but I can do nothing for him. I stay in Delhi because I have begun to know what pain it means to be a woman. Mummy says I matured so early because she must have fed me too much meat — I am forbidden to eat any more kukris, or to go alone in the car with Nand Singh. She says I complain too much every month and Nancy's chauffeur delivers a box of imported Kotex after Dad is posted away again, this time to Bangalore.

I think our eucalyptus must be a girl-tree; it takes too much from the soil and leaves everything around it parched and angry. The sparrows mate and push their young to fly. I wonder if the one Dad shot had a mate, and did he miss her? Did she have a young sparrow?

I wander into Dad's empty room and take the key to his almirah from beneath his pillow. A few minutes later the battered old attaché case lies open before me and I look at Chandini Kaur's face again. And at the muslin-wrapped triangular bundle. But now I see there is more. A yellowed letter with a Government of India stamp. The date on the letter: August 28, 1948 — twelve months after Partition.

"I am the concerned social worker who has located your sister, Chandini Kaur, formerly of village Thamali, District Rawalpindi. She has recovered from her abduction and is now in good health. By the grace of God, she gave birth in Sargodha to a healthy boy. She requests you to receive her as soon as possible. The Government of India Ministry of Relief and Rehabilitation will pay for her journey if you will acknowledge . . . ," then a post office at which to write to a woman now known as Jehanara Begum.

I hold the letter against the slight rise of my chest in gratitude. Dad did not kill his sister. I tell myself I knew it all along. How can I have been so base, so vile, so ungrateful a daughter as to have let such a thought enter my mind? He was just preparing us, as a father must in a time of war, for all that he could foresee. And Inder: how could I have been so silly as to think he was serious when he said, "I will." He was just playing at being a man, as he always does. I must have imagined his avoidance afterward. Mummy always says I am such a fear-filled girl, it will be difficult to find me a good family.

I read the letter again, but this time I come away with questions. If she was in good health in 1948, what happened to her? Who would know? And who will be willing to tell me? I must know. She looks up at me as though she wants me to find out.

Too slow for my patience, my hands fumble putting the Moonlight Princess back in her case, the case back in the almirah. I smooth Dad's clothes inside.

Nand Singh is washing the car in the driveway, snow-white turban bobbing over its olive green tubbiness. I hunker down and wait next to the bucket of soapy water so he knows I want his advice as my elder and do not wish to play mem-sahib today. He gives the car a final caress and joins me, asking after my health, calling me beti. I call him "Nand Singhji" to show my respect as I answer so he will understand my seriousness.

I say, "Do you know the story of my aunt, Chandini Kaur?" I say it as though I always knew I had an aunt.

He answers warily, "There are many stories of Chandini Kaur."

I prompt, "The trouble with stories is that some are true and some are not."

"There are people in the world who spread false stories."

"You are not one of them, so I have come to you."

"I am your servant. Command me."

He is humouring me. The only person I know who commands Nand Singh to do anything at all is Dad. I take a deep breath.

"I want to know if she is alive."

"Her body may be alive."

"What do you mean?"

"Her name was never to be spoken again in this house. I am surprised you know anything about her. For your father, she is dead."

"How did she die for my father?"

"She was abducted by the Muslims who invaded Thamali village in 1947."

"This I know," I lie. I make my breath come slower. I do not look at him. "But how did she die for my father?"

He looks confused and repeats as though I have not heard, "She was abducted by Musalmaan." This time, he uses the Punjabi form of the word so that even someone as slow as a girl-child may understand.

"But she was found again."

"They found a woman whose name was Jehanara Begum and who said she was your father's sister, Chandini Kaur."

"Yes. Go on."

"It was a lie, of course."

"Why do you say that?"

"Any sister of your father's would have died before allowing herself to be called Jehanara Begum."

"Then — you met her?"

"Ji Huzoor. Your father sent me to give her money."

"Why did you not bring her back?"

He seems about to lose patience. "She was dead for your father."

"Did he not love her?"

"Of course. All brothers love their sisters."

"Then why could she not return with you?" Tears for a woman in a withered photograph are forming behind my eyes.

"Because no woman of your father's family would have allowed herself to become a Musalmaan and then to have a Musalmaan's child. So I came back and agreed with your father that she must be an imposter, for she couldn't possibly be his sister . . ." He shifts his weight from one shiny black shoe heel to the other. "Who knows, maybe she was mad, maybe she wanted a share of this house he got in compensation for Thamali, or who knows what she wanted . . ."

"Did you not recognize her?"

"My memory of her was a year old. I could not be sure."

The man whose memory is a household legend tilts his turban to the sky. I try again.

"She had a son."

"Mmhmm." The wrinkles in his forehead disappear into the line of his turban.

"What happened to her son?"

"The offspring of that Musalmaan bastard died, God be thanked."

He rises to his feet, picks up a polishing rag and begins rubbing the radiator grill. But I am not finished asking.

"How?"

"One day she was bathing it, and it stayed underwater too long."

It stayed underwater? A baby doesn't stay underwater.

The polishing motion stops, his brown hand stayed by memory.

"Then again this Jehanara Begum wrote to your father, saying the baby was gone now and again asking to be taken back."

"And what did he say?"

"What could he say? He sent her money, told her his sister was dead and he was sorry for her troubles and to trouble him no more."

"Then?"

"She should have taken her own life when she had her wits — I heard she became mad. Completely pagal. Now . . . it has been many years now, no letters."

He walks around to the other side of the car and renews his efforts to polish its already gleaming surface. I pick up five round, smooth stones from the garden and throw a listless round of punj-gitra. With my right hand, I throw a big stone in the air and pick up one stone at a time from the remaining four. The first stone is for a woman whose name meant Moonlight, the second for the Muslim who took her by force, the third is for a baby who stayed underwater too long and the fourth . . . the big stone hits the ground before my hand can pick up the fourth. The fourth and fifth are for a brother and his mad sister, partitioned by family ties.

Inder comes back from boarding school and shows me a pack of imported cigarettes. I can't believe he is touching them with his bare hands. I am sure something terrible will happen to him; I remind him that Guru Gobind Singh forbade us to smoke. He says he no longer cares about Guru Gobind Singh because Guru Gobind Singh doesn't care about him. He takes the cigarettes and hides them between the pages of my schoolbooks. I feel sure everyone will smell them in my schoolbag.

I say, "If you smoke you will become an impure Sikh and then Dad will say you are not his son."

Inder laughs in a new way, an ugly way I have never seen before.

"Dad won't say that — I am his only son." And now there is a sneer in his voice, a sneer for me. "If *you* tried it, you'd be dead."

I back away. I don't like his tone.

"And if you tell, I'll kill you." He makes it sound so simple, like the chicken-seller killing the little kukri.

His eyes wander towards Dad's closet and rest there ever so fleetingly. He was given permission. He was told I belong to him, that he has the power to will me to live or to die.

I say, "Don't talk that way, Inder. I am your sister, and I love you." Even to my own ears my voice sounds a whine.

"No one loves anyone else in this family. It's all a show."

"I do. I love you."

"What does your love matter? You're just a girl."

I let the tears come as I ponder his words under the eucalyptus tree. He's right. I'll be twelve soon, and my love or hate, bravery or fear doesn't matter. All that he and I have in common now is blood and honour.

I pick up my skipping rope to begin the thousand skips a day
Mummy prescribes for me to lose weight —
Miss Lucy had a baby, she named him Tiny Tim.
She put him in the bathtub to see if he could swim . . .
If I had a Muslim baby, would I have the courage to drown it?

Mummy says she's had to become the family's bootlegger because,
she says, drinking Indian whiskey is too dangerous; you never
know what dangerous poison is mixed in there. So she does fa-
vours for Nancy and Pierre — invites Nancy to her kitty parties,
sends her the Chinese hairdresser girl before a High Commission
party, orders French bread for Pierre at the Akbar Hotel bakery,
and has her tailor sew Nancy's sundresses — until she can suggest, "If you insist . . . a bottle of whiskey, then." When Dad is
in Delhi again, Mummy invites Nancy and Pierre to dinner and
orders the cook to make western food — mushrooms and broc-
coli, expensive things we never usually eat.

I wear one of Mummy's old salwar kameezes, altered to my
size so that I don't need to hide my naked legs as I try to do in my
school skirt. Nancy and Pierre arrive with a bottle of Cutty Sark,
and I think they don't notice that Dad and Mummy don't talk
directly to one another or that Inder coughs his persistent irri-
tating cough and yawns without putting his hand to his mouth
while Dad talks about wanting to send him to college in Canada.
Pierre suggests the University of Montreal, but Dad says he wants
Inder to go to an English-speaking university like the University
of Toronto so Inder will be able to come back and continue
Dad's work, developing India. Pierre says he thinks Quebec is
like Pakistan, a place that needs to be cut apart from Canada as
Pakistan was carved away from India. Dad falls quiet after that.
I eat very little and refuse the caramel custard.

Mummy remarks how limp my hair is, and the next day Nancy's

chauffeur delivers two bottles of Flex Balsam shampoo and a new hair dryer, which Mummy takes and sets aside for my trousseau. I have to use the shampoo every two days to make my hair thick so that someone will marry me.

Mummy begins to give Inder more pocket money and says it is his duty to look after her when she gets old. For me, she spends two hundred rupees on a contraption that hangs from our bedroom door and says I must swing against it every day to try and grow taller. Inder watches me with blank smoke-glazed eyes, and now he hides his slender hand-rolled cigarettes and a pill box in Dad's attaché case in the almirah with Chandini Kaur's picture so no one will know. He fights with Nand Singh, who will not yet let him drive the Ambassador alone, and makes friends of the now-gawky jhuggi boys Mummy always forbade him to play with. They bring him paan leaves that do not smell of the usual spices and betelnut, stuffed with things that he says melt on his tongue. Hippies come to meet him in the gully behind the house, but he says they only ask him directions to American Express. There are nights when he has bad trips: his hands are going away from him while Dad and Mummy and I are all trying to kill him. Despite the heat, I cover him with blankets to muffle his giggles and cries; Miss Shafi has to wake me in class most days. The first time he gets a beating from Dad, it's for flunking a chemistry test. The second time, it's for cheating. The third time, it's for drinking all the Cutty Sark Nancy and Pierre brought.

Miss Shafi teaches me history this year and I find out that her first name is Raza. She has a boyfriend now and he wears a Levi's jacket and rides a black and silver Rajdoot motorcycle. After school, I see her put her arm around his waist as he kicks it into motion, her two dainty sandals dangling above the exhaust. When I tell Mummy they are in love, she slaps her forehead and says Miss Shafi must be a poor nautch-girl with parents who do not love her enough to care about her reputation.

Miss Shafi gives us a history test and we have to write about Gandhi's Quit India movement and Nehru and India's Tryst with Destiny. "On the stroke of midnight when the world sleeps, India will awake . . . " She tells us she has relatives who escaped India and went to Pakistan and they too rode the death trains.

I want — how I want — to tell her about the Moonlight Princess, to ask her if her relatives in Pakistan might know her. But I have learned, learned that to be part of a family you have to agree to keep its secrets. Because there are penalties to be paid by kukris who crow. After all, there is nothing in my history book about one Chandini Kaur who became Jehanara Begum and who is dead for my father and mad besides, nor any woman like her.

Now I am thirteen. Nand Singh prepares the car for Inder to drive as though he were doing it for Mummy or Dad; it does not occur to either Inder or me to bring our friends home. Inder is old enough to have his own room and there is no one to muffle his nightmares now. We share a bathroom, where I find a sick-sweet smell, syringes hidden behind a rusty pipe, and cigarette ash like bird-droppings, but still Mummy refers to him as "Inderji" when talking to the cook and tries to tempt his nonexistent appetite with everything from imported Camembert cheese to Swiss chocolates. He keeps the large doses of pocket money coming, saying he needs it to buy imported acne cream, and she tells me daily how he will be the one to look after her when she gets old and I am finally off her hands. I watch Nand Singh let Inder bump the old car out of the driveway and drive off without me. Now he's a seller as well as a buyer.

Everything is blurred in school although I sit at the front of the class, and Miss Shafi sends a note to tell Mummy I may need glasses. Mummy unfolds the note slowly before me and when she has read it there are tears.

"How will anyone marry you now, you ungrateful child."

She summons the car, and it is an emergency so Nand Singh drives as only a Sikh driver can, one hand on the horn, emerging victorious from a mêlée of garbage-grazing cows and bicycles and buses to park in front of a whitewashed private clinic. Mummy waits in the back seat ignoring beggars and bargaining for strawberries while my lashes catch in the doctor's eye-tester and the judgement is made: I will need glasses. When I return to the car with the news, she is distraught. A girl with glasses is more difficult to marry off than a fatty. All the way home, she asks what she has done to deserve this. She says her family has never had weak eyes — Dad, on the other hand, she remembers, has many relatives with weak eyes.

I ask in English so that Nand Singh will not understand, "Did Chandini Kaur have weak eyes?"

She stops in mid-sentence.

"That's enough from you. Don't give me any more back-chat."

But Chandini Kaur must have had weak eyes not to see when her son was drowning.

When Mummy and Daddy and Inder return from the doctor, Dad takes Inder up to the terrace for another thrashing. They are up there a long time while Mummy and I sit in cane chairs under the eucalyptus tree and let dusk fall around us. We listen to the whop-whop of Dad's belt and Inder's cries, "I'm sorry, I'm sorry. I'll never do it again."

"He's getting it from the hippies," she says.

"He'd get it anyway." I say.

"How do you know?" with one of her suspicious looks.

"Everyone knows." I shrug.

"Don't shrug. You'll get round shoulders. Has he ever tried to give you some?"

"No."

It doesn't comfort her.

"My only son," she says. "What have I not given him? He doesn't even talk properly anymore — he gets confused in the middle of a sentence or he laughs in the middle of any discussion. It's impossible to take him anywhere with my friends. Who will look after me when I get old? Listen to him . . ."

Inder's cries dissolve into weeping.

Mummy continues, "Everyone can hear our shame . . . we will never be able to get you married."

"I never want to be married."

"Don't be silly."

Dad emerges, massaging his wrist.

"He says he will never take it again." False certitude reverberates in his voice. His eyes are full of tears for a son who has slipped away.

"What did the doctor say?" I ask.

"The doctor is a fool," says my father. "Probably foreign-returned. Gave me some bukvaas about going to see a psychiatrist. I told him, My son is not mad. Psychiatrists are for madness."

A sparrow titters.

In a moment he says, "After all, we have never had any madness in our family."

This is what I must remember if ever I am asked. We have never had any madness in our family.

Above us, luminescent and reproachful, a woman-face moon dangles like a pendant on the breast of the dissipating day.

Gayatri

Gayatri had been cocooned in a sulk for two days now. She wove it, look by look, spinning it slowly, clenching its threads around everyone, ominous and accusing. She took it to bed with her, using its coolness to shut out the night heat instead of the new electric khus-khus cooler. She pulled a sheet up over her head and stayed sulking till the heat of a new Delhi morning panted like a waiting dog outside the chic-bamboo curtains. Now she sat at her dressing table, eying her husband like a mynah bird from under perfectly arched eyebrows.

"Reena brought Alphonso mangoes, specially for you, from Bombay," he coaxed.

Mentioning Reena was a mistake. The eyebrows met in the middle, and Gayatri turned away. "She's your sister, she brought them for you. Go eat them."

He sighed. "She's come to stay and you've not even offered her a glass of water, Gayatri."

"If she needs water, she has only to ask the servant. I'm the elder by six years. Let her touch my feet first."

He took off his sandals and sat cross-legged on her bed. "She's a modern girl. She doesn't even touch my father's feet, let alone

31

yours. Besides, you two used to get along like true sisters before
—what's all this bad feeling, I say?"

Gayatri didn't answer. She opened a jar of Orange Skin Cream
and started to massage it into the complexion her parents' advertisement had described as "wheatish" in colour. He watched her
sulk a little longer — she'd given him two sons, so she was due
at least that much. Then he rose, adjusting his Peshawri salwar,
and called to the sleepy-eyed servant boy to serve the Alphonso
mangoes for his breakfast.

She looks like a hippie, Gayatri thought. Those faded jeans and
long silver earrings and that awful rust-brown kurta. Today she
wore one anklet, and such was her irritation that Gayatri resisted
the urge to tell her she had lost its mate. She had the usual cloth
satchel over her shoulder and Gayatri thought she could smell
cigarettes.

"Hi, Guy." Reena draped her long legs over the side of a cane
moora.

She wanted to say, Don't call me Guy, but it was beneath her.

"Are you feeling well? I came in last night and you were already
asleep. You know I got a job, don't you?"

"I know."

"What do you know about it? Tell me."

"You're going to be working for an airline."

"No, no, Guy. Get it right, yar. I'm going to be an air hostess —
I mean, a stewardess."

Gayatri lashed out. "Haan, haan, next you'll become a model,
or maybe a nachnewali."

Reena cocked her head to one side and regarded her in some
astonishment. "Guy, what's the matter? You should be happy for
me. I'll be making two thousand rupees a month and flying all
over the world."

But Gayatri was not impressed.

"Serving men in the sky or on the ground — what's the difference? If it's money you want, I could give you money if your brother can't do his duty and support you. My parents gave me enough. Why should a girl from a good family need to work?"

Reena laughed. "So what would you like me to do after college instead? Advertise for a husband, like you did?"

Gayatri adjusted her French chiffon sari with dignity. "I did not advertise, my parents advertised. And what is so wrong with that, please?"

"Well, if there is no difference between a stewardess and a dance girl, there is no difference between your parents' advertising and your advertising."

Gayatri took refuge in righteousness.

"Your parents and your brother spoil you too much, Reena. So much so that you think you're independent now. When I was in college there were some girls like you who went wild, and then their families had to find them *any* match, because their reputation was ruined. And of course then the whole family suffers. Well, maybe this job will be a good pastime until they find a suitable boy for you."

Reena uncoiled from the moora and stretched. "You know, Guy, I think you're jealous."

Gayatri sent her one of her Looks. Reena pretended to be oblivious.

"I think you'd love to travel and meet people — different people. You're just afraid of what it might do to our precious family reputation, na?"

Gayatri was quiet; the sulk was waiting to descend, but Reena continued. "You've done your duty now — two boys, both very spoiled. Why don't you get a job, see the world, start a business? All you do while Ramesh is at Glaxo is to haggle with the fruit merchants and watch American movies on the video. Aren't you bored?"

Gayatri allowed herself to smile. "Of course I'm bored. If I had been interested in working, my parents could have found me a poor man. But since they wanted me to marry a rich man, they protected me so I had a perfect reputation when I married your brother. My mother always said, 'A girl can't be too careful with her reputation.'"

Reena reached over her shoulder and picked up a bottle of Worth from the dressing table and sprayed a little on Gayatri's neck. "Smell that, Guy. I want a man who loves Reena to enjoy that perfume on my body, not a man who wants a cow to give him calves."

"I don't understand you anymore, Reena. You've become a very selfish girl. I think your brother and your parents will all be sorry we did not stop you when we could."

Reena shot back, "Not a selfish girl, Guy. A selfish woman." Then, more gently, "Guy, think about it. You love me, I know — you're not usually nasty. I really think you're jealous, so you're talking as if you're eighty-four years old."

Gayatri's sulk descended. Her sister-in-law tried to meet her eyes in the mirror, but her crescent-moon eyelids declared the conversation was over. Perfume from the open bottle mixed with the fragrance of marigolds as Reena lifted the chic. Gayatri felt the heat blast inward and red sun-swirls form behind her tight-shut eyes.

The children were at school when Reena called. The servant boy brought the cordless phone into Gayatri's room on a silver tray, but he didn't quite know what to do after he had presented it to her. Gayatri waved him into a squat on the floor.

"I have a layover in Delhi for twenty-four hours," Reena said. "I'm staying at the Ashoka Hotel. Would you like to come and have some chai? They serve great pastries, too."

"I just had breakfast, Reena."

"Well, I wanted to introduce you to a friend."

Gayatri was immediately suspicious.

"Male or female?"

"Male."

"Ramesh and I could come this evening for drinks." It would never do to meet Ramesh's sister in a hotel in company with a male friend. It might look like endorsement, encouragement, approval.

"He's very nice, and I thought you'd like to meet him."

"Reena, don't do anything stupid, now."

"I told you he's very nice, and he's a friend. What do you mean, do anything stupid?"

Gayatri felt she was deliberately being obtuse.

"I mean, don't do anything your family would be ashamed of."

Reena's voice was a little sad. "Listen, you're more conservative than my parents, Guy. By the way, he's American."

"I'm relieved."

"Relieved?"

"Mmm. They sleep with women, but they don't marry them." Reena's voice rose a little.

"So, are you saying it's all right for him to sleep with me, but not to marry me?"

"Better for your reputation, Reena. I'm only being practical. If you will go off and sow your wild seeds, it's probably better to do it with an American. He won't know anyone in our crowd, so you're pretty safe."

"Gayatri, maybe I don't want to be safe. Maybe I want to live."

"Rubbish."

"So, will you come and meet him?"

"Leave it open. Ramesh and I may drop by this evening for drinks."

She placed the phone back on the waiting tray. There was no reason to bother Ramesh — he would only worry. Besides, it gave her pleasure to think of Reena and her male friend waiting in suspense. It might cramp the American's style. Maybe Reena was right. Perhaps she was just a little jealous.

The company wives declared Gayatri's bridge party a success. The stupid little servant boy was quite worn out from carrying tea and samosas and Bavarian cream torte to each in turn. Once she'd scolded him for letting a blob of strawberry ice cream fall on the oriental carpet, Gayatri felt her housewifely duties were done and she could sink into the leather armchair and turn on the video in air-conditioned comfort. Only then did she pick up the letter from Reena.

When she finished reading it, she called Ramesh at the office. It took her about half an hour to get through to him, even with the redial button.

"Ramesh, I just got a letter from Reena."

"Yes, any problem?"

"Yes. She says she has gotten married."

"To whom?"

"Some American fellow."

"Oh, what is his name?"

"I don't know. What does it matter? My parents would have died of shame if I had married an American." An explosion was in order, threats to kill, to poison, to maim, or, at the very least, never to speak to his ingrate sister again. This would be appropriate to Reena's provocation, to the sheer audacity with which she had flaunted her independence from her family's opinion. This is how Gayatri's family would have reacted if she had ever done or thought of committing such an act. Why, if she'd even dreamed of such folly, she would not be Ramesh's wife today.

She heard Ramesh laugh. "Well, times have changed, Gayatri. Your parents didn't have such a lot of money, so reputation was very important. Now in Reena's case, no one will dare to say much. And who knows, an American brother-in-law can be an asset also. I am only sorry she got married without telling us, but she must have had her reasons. Did she say if they plan to have a Hindu ceremony as well?

Gayatri's angry, hot tears were falling on the letter.

"No . . . no. She didn't say."

"Any picture?"

She hadn't thought to look. "Yes, here's a picture."

"Well, what does he look like?"

Gayatri held it up triumphantly, as if Ramesh could see through the phone.

"He's a black man."

Ramesh was quiet for a long time.

She waited.

Then she heard, "She will need all the help we can give her. Send her a telegram, Gayatri. Say Congratulations. Oh, and Gayatri . . ."

"Yes?"

"Sign it: Love, Ramesh and Gayatri."

Simran

AMRIT

Veeru and I had dinner at the Delhi Gymkhana Club around midnight and then drove to greet Simran at Palam airport. I was the first to find her as we peered through the glass wall smeared by the breath of waiting friends and relatives. She looked bright and alive despite a twenty-six-hour plane ride, and she'd put on a little weight in just four months in America. I was glad to see she was excited to see us. In America, children learn that they can blame their parents for everything and then they all, parents and children, spend years in psychotherapy. I felt so relieved to see her I was almost in tears. Which mother wouldn't worry about a nineteen-year-old unmarried daughter so far away?

She asked questions about everyone as if she had been away a year and I was glad to notice she had not caught an American accent. (I have *always* tried to teach my pupils to speak the Queen's English.) When we got home, she went around the house touching everything familiar as if to reassure herself that it was all just as she left it. Although it was four in the morning by then, she wanted Veeru to put some brandy in her hot milk and Ovaltine just as he did when she was a child.

I listened with every nerve to her excited, animated chatter.

I was determined to notice any signs of change in her. I had good reason. Every time we called (person to person calls, three minutes, cost a hundred rupees) she was "out." Yet in every letter she said she was studying hard and taking our advice to stay clear of Americans and make friends with other foreign students.. She'd always been addicted to books, but we were troubled by the constant excuse, "I was at the library." I've never known a library that stayed open till midnight and we go to some of the best libraries in Delhi.

It was Kanti, who's been with our family now for almost fourteen years, who found the first thing that made me worry. She was unpacking Simran's suitcases and she held up a clothbound volume, asking where Simran wanted her to place it. I said, "Let me see that."

When I realized that it was a copy of the Koran that lay cradled in my only daughter's baggage, I was horrified. What had my daughter exposed herself to in America? We are a proud Sikh family and we have long memories. Our Gurus were tortured to death by Moghul rulers only three hundred years ago, and both Veeru's father and mine still get tears in their eyes talking about the fate of old Sikh friends and neighbours at the hands of Muslim marauders during the 1947 partition. Veeru is even old enough to remember the sight of Sikh women, raped and disgraced by Muslims, walking home to Amritsar. And my daughter comes back from America with a copy of the Koran? I don't know what is in it — I only know it is the book that gave its believers permission to kill us. Out loud, I said sternly, "I do not want this book in my house."

"Oh, Mummy, how silly. It's just a present I got from a friend when I was leaving for the winter break. What's so terrible about it?"

"What's so terrible? Ask your father. See if he'll allow this in our house."

"C'mon, Mumji. I've read the Bible and the Gita, too. Just because you read something doesn't mean you have to believe it; just because you read something doesn't mean it's true. You really should be more tolerant. Have you read it?"

"Don't say 'come on' to me. Of course I haven't read it. All I can say is, you better not let your father see it."

She was about to argue but thought better of it. It was her first night home, after all. She nudged Kanti aside and began unpacking herself as if she were Kanti's servant and not the other way around. I said, "You're not in America anymore, you don't have to do everything yourself. Let Kanti do it or you will make her upset."

She said, "I'm looking for the presents I brought back." And soon, forgetting our little tussles, she had them spread on the bed. A length of cloth for a salwar kameez for me, polyester with a self-design (I think about eight dollars per yard), a tie for Veeru (about twenty dollars, not a brand name I recognized, but he thought it was an excellent choice), a box of chocolates for her brother away at boarding school in Dehradun (maybe ten dollars), and — she's picked up the American habit of spoiling the servants — a sari length for Kanti that must have cost at least fifty dollars.

I said, "Don't be so generous — give her the box of chocolates."

She grinned mischievously, "And give the sari to Raju?"

"No — we'll find him something else."

"I'm only joking."

"I know your kind of joking."

We settled on a bottle of hand lotion for Kanti instead, but I lay next to Veeru with a sense of apprehension afterwards, watching the winter sun rise over my roses and chrysanthemums as the mali tended them outside our window. Finally, I told him what I found in her luggage. He was appalled, as I knew he would be — all he kept saying was, "My daughter? My daughter reading the Koran?" He would not sleep till I promised to watch Simran carefully for signs that she might be in danger of becoming a Muslim.

MIRZA

You couldn't miss Simran sitting on that bar stool in the residence hall lounge because she was a splash of red, gold and orange in a room full of faded jeans, sweatshirts and denim jackets. She had the panicked look of a recently arrived foreign student, and I knew she came from some convent girls' school in Pakistan or India from the way she shrank backwards every time a man walked too close. She sipped her drink looking over the top of the glass, huge fish-shaped eyes darting from one speaker to another.

I was in love before I crossed the room to ask her name, introduce myself as Mirza, the head of the Pakistani Cultural Society, and ask her which part of the subcontinent she was from. When she said Delhi, India, I hesitated a bit. Then I asked, "Did your family originally come from Pakistan before 1947?"

"Yes," she said. "Lahore."

"Lahore! My family is from Lahore, too."

They weren't, but I was in love, so they had to be.

She looked relieved, moving a little on the bar stool, just enough so that I heard the chink of glass bangles and noticed she had painted toenails. I hadn't seen a woman with bangles or painted toenails in North Carolina in two years — all the time I'd been there. I praised Allah, most benevolent, ever merciful, for rewarding me by sending her.

I have to say she made no attempt to be artful. She simply managed to fill my entire mind within ten minutes. I listened to her demure talk about coming to America to learn computer science and thought, "You don't know ishk yet, meri jaan. When you learn ishk you will forget computer science and nothing but love will enter your mind."

Aloud, I said, "It is very refreshing to find a woman from our part of the world who is interested in such important topics as computer science. Progress depends on women's education, I have always said." Of course, I had said nothing of the kind, ever, but that was what she wanted to hear so I said it. And I added casually, "You know, I am a computer science major too — just a few years ahead of you, that's all."

She was impressed. I could see it from the way she looked at my glasses with a new respect. I am not as tall as most men from Pakistan, and my hair is already thinning slightly though I'm only twenty-one, but I straightened up to my full height and said, "Just call me if you have any trouble with your classes at all."

And I took the opportunity to give her my phone number and get hers. Then as I advised her about the different Indian and Pakistani cultural groups and expounded on how Indians and Pakistanis are friends in America, the American students left us alone as usual in a little island surrounded by ignorance, and together we watched them become steadily less and less inhibited. She showed a most proper disgust, and if I thought she could have been a little less curious I kept it to myself. A red-haired fellow lurched too close and I said, assuming a slight accent, "You gotta watch out for these guys."

Over the next few weeks, I made myself indispensable to her. I advised her on everything, whether I knew anything about it or not. My older brother always said, "You have to make them think you know more than they do, or you don't get their respect." I also know the promise of protection is the easiest way to seduce a woman — at least, any woman from my part of the world. So I offered her mine.

I showed her how to use a cash machine (I was glad she didn't ask how the damned thing worked, because I couldn't have told her), explained the phone system so that she could call home, introduced her to the transient world of international students as if she were my personal property . . . and very soon everyone thought she *was* my property. All but Simran herself.

If only I had known then — she was bent on driving me mad.

AMRIT

She had been home only a few days when I began to notice she'd started doing some strange things. Keeping a diary, for instance. I began to watch what I said to her because I was getting the feeling she was going to write it all down in that diary. It was as if she was studying us, looking at us as if she'd never seen us before, questioning, questioning everything. I said, "Simran, it's really not ladylike to ask so many questions."

"Not ladylike, Mummy!" She let out a peal of laughter. Was it my imagination, or did she laugh a lot more and louder since she came home? Even her limbs imitated American indiscipline; her gestures were wider, and when she wore a sari I was dismayed that she no longer walked with a graceful glide, but strode as firmly as any shameless blonde woman. For this I sent her to America?

I found some comfort in the thought that her behaviour did not seem to be that of a woman who wishes to convert to Islam.

MIRZA

Try as I might, Simran never seemed conscious of the fact that I am a man. The same girl who told a friend she felt uncomfortable talking to a male professor without the door of his office open or another woman present regarded me as if I was an amusing younger brother. She allowed me to bring her laddoos from an Indian store in Raleigh, and to buy her chocolates from Woolworth without attaching any significance to my actions. I started buying more expensive gifts, as if my job in the Union cafeteria made me a millionaire. Did she need film to send pictures home to her Mummy and Daddy? I bought her a dozen. Did she not have a poster for her little dorm room? I bought one for her. Did she need a calculator? I held forth for an hour on the relative merits of different brands and then I ran out and bought her the most expensive one.

I always knew where to find her — wrapped in a shawl in a corner study carrel on the third floor of the library, reading and reading as if her life depended on it. The books she was reading had nothing to do with computer science — I can't remember what they were, but I'm sure they must have been where she learned the tricks that she used later to drive me to do the things I did.

The semester was coming to an end when she told me her parents had decided they could afford to spend the money for her to fly home for the three-week break. I was distraught. No warning. No discussion of how I might be feeling. No concern for my well-being while she was gone. No "Mirza, how will you survive?" All she said was, "If I wasn't going back to India, I'd take a train and go all over looking at this country, talking to everyone, everyone along the way. Why don't you do that, Mirza? It might be fun!"

Sometimes she really made me angry with her suggestions. Why didn't I do that? Because the only country I would want to explore would be Pakistan — that's the only country that is beautiful. And besides, having spent all my money on her, I didn't have much left to go anywhere over the three-week break. Instead, I would stay on the empty campus in my room, as I'd done many times before — only this time I would have her to wait for.

But would she wait for me? I began to worry. She was nineteen years old. I asked some friends in the Pakistani Cultural Society and they thought Sikh women are usually married by the time they are twenty. Could it be that her parents wanted her to return to India to be engaged or married? It would, after all, be wiser if she were not dangling before every man's nose in this fashion. I thought I must tell her my feelings and discuss — what? — marriage? I suppose so. But somehow I had a difficult time imagining her, a Sikh, married to me.

A few days before she left, taking the Amtrak train to New York to fly home, I gave her an English translation of the Koran. I don't know what she thought when I gave it to her — all I know is that she treated it like all my gifts before; she was too kind to refuse them but she could not imagine the feeling that drove me to give her anything — everything. I walked back to my cell in the dorm and picked up the campus directory. Idly, I looked up her name and noted that her permanent address and phone number in Delhi were listed. I copied them carefully — as though I were in any danger of forgetting them once I had seen them! Then I sat down to write love poetry to my oblivious beloved.

AMRIT

Veeru is not accustomed to being challenged in his own household, and that, too, by his daughter. Almost in the first week she was home they began to argue regularly, and it made me anxious about her future. I told him we should try and introduce her to some nice families, maybe get her engaged before she went back to America. In my way of thinking, he'd brought it on himself by wanting her to have this American degree. I never studied in America, and I have been content because I have always known instinctively and naturally just how far I can push the men around me, when to be winsome, when to be silent, when to become visibly sick with internal pain rather than unbecomingly obstinate. In four months in "the States," as she called it, Simran had lost all restraint, all decorum.

I had always been careful to find out what she was reading and to know what she was thinking. I'd bought some of her books myself — introduced her to great literature: Sir Walter Scott, Lord Tennyson, Oscar Wilde, Jane Austen, the Brontës and Charles Dickens. But now I felt shut out as I looked at the titles she was reading — all American sidewalk psychology and all this American liberty theory that only America with all its land and so few people can afford. I didn't want her to spend her time shopping like all her old friends from college in Delhi did till they were decently married off, but it is a big responsibility to have an unmarried daughter, and I didn't want to be blamed if she went astray.

I'll never forget the moment I knew she had betrayed our trust, the money we had wasted on her education, the way we had borne the dire predictions of our friends in sending her abroad to study. All in one moment, I knew we had created a monster, an ungrateful, rebellious, selfish monster and we had no one to blame but ourselves. The knowledge came to me the moment I picked up the telephone and heard a male voice interspersed with static say, "May I please speak to Simran?"

I said, "She is not here."

And I slammed the receiver back on the hook. I saw Kanti looking at me with surprise from the kitchen and I said shortly, "Wrong number."

I had to protect my daughter's reputation.

MIRZA

I had only been in Grand Central Station once before, when I arrived in the States and took the train to Raleigh two years ago.

It's a comforting place for me, grimy and garish with lots of beggars — Americans call them "homeless people" — just like home. I had taken advantage of a Christmas discount and traced my beloved's last journey to this place. I don't know what I had in mind going there — it just seemed better to leave the campus than spend my time listening for the tinkle of glass bangles, lying in her spot on the third floor of the library.

I decided to get some coffee (Americans have no idea how to make tea) and a donut. It's a strange thing about donuts. Americans have twenty names for the different kinds of donuts, more than they have for the relationships in their families. So I just pointed when the girl at the counter asked what kind I wanted. She looked at me nervously. I suppose my eyes looked a little bloodshot — I had been trying to stay awake at the same time as my Simran and sleep at the same time as she did, too.

I sat in the glass booth dubbed a café, gazing past a long line of telephones, and afterwards I would have taken my return ticket and wandered back to the platform for the Raleigh train, but I felt a tap on my shoulder and some fellow with a Yankees jacket over baggy corduroy trousers said in Urdu, "Are you from India or Pakistan?" I drew myself up proudly and said, "Pakistan."

"I too am from Pakistan," he said, lapsing into English. And he placed his tray on the table next to mine and slipped into the seat beside me so we both sat looking outward at the great hall milling with people.

"In Pakistan there would be many more people at a train station," I mused, companionably.

"You are missing home?" he said sympathetically.

"Yes, of course," I said, not without a twinge of guilt, for I really hadn't thought of my family ever since I met my new love.

"You want to call home? I have a credit card."

"You are very kind, but how could I use your credit card?"

I was somewhat surprised. We Pakistanis usually have a little less trust of strangers than he exhibited. Usually we will at least ask one another's village of origin before offering hospitality.

"Well, it is not really my credit card," he explained. "It is a credit card number you can use for the phone. And then you can call anywhere you like and never have to pay." His glee began to remind me of an American TV commercial, so I stopped him with a line I'd heard them use. "So what's the catch?"

He closed his eyes with all the sanctimony of a Christian at prayer and said, "Allah is my witness, no catch. Here, you go and try the number. If your call goes through you can pay me only ten dollars — not even enough for one call, leave alone all the calls you can make for free with this number."

I knew I was placing myself in danger. I was a computer science major — did he think I didn't know how easy it is to trace a call with a bum credit card? But my obsession was strong in me and I yearned for one syllable of Simran's voice, so I made my way to the phones and tried the call, billing it as swiftly as my fingers could enter the code to some fat rich American who could well afford it.

I followed the phone call in my mind, hearing the static rush over the Atlantic, felt it cross Europe, dance over the Khyber pass and drop through Pakistan, bridging the winter-dry riverbeds of the Jhelum, the Chenab, the Ravi, the Sutlej, the Beas, finally swooping down to the plains of Delhi. I felt it sidle into Simran's house. There was a ringing, trr-trr trr-trr. Someone — was it Simran? — said, "Hello?"

And then I said, voice cracking like a schoolboy, "May I please speak to Simran?" I felt as though I would choke.

"She is not here," said the voice that was Simran's and yet not Simran's. And then, click. That was all. And the risk I had taken to call her brushed aside, the sacrifice I had made in following her to Grand Central ignored. Any minute I could be arrested. I would tell them then, "It was all for her. The woman tempted me, arrest her, that wanton harlot!"

None of this passed my lips. I had the credit card and I would call again.

I went back to my new friend and gladly paid him ten dollars, saying, "It worked but I will not try that again. Once is enough, mia. I don't want to get caught."

He said knowingly, "As you please. Consider it a gift — just a small tofah — in case of emergency."

Then he was gone, and I took the train back to Raleigh. By the time I got back to my empty, silent room, I could stand my thoughts no longer, and so I ran out again to the pay phone at the corner convenience store and tried to call my heartless love again.

AMRIT

My daughter seems intent on ruining this family. I went into her bedroom and had a talk with her after that call, asking her, "Who is this man who thinks he can call you in your parents' home?"

She looked so surprised and so innocent, and she said, "Mummy, I don't know who it can be. Did he say his name?"

But I was not born yesterday and I said, "How did he get your number?"

She looked worried and said simply, "I don't know."

"What do you mean you don't know? So he just dreamed it or what? Ten o'clock at night and he thinks he has the right to call you?" I was beginning to sound shrill, but I was frightened for her. Better that she should get a taste of my anger first, for Veeru would not spare her.

"Mummy, maybe it's important — why didn't you let me speak? I would have told you what it was about."

"Let you speak! That man didn't have an American accent,

my dear, he had . . ." I searched for the right words but my fears made me say, "he had a Muslim accent."

Then she laughed. Laughed in my face as if my fears were nothing. "Oh, that must be Mirza," she said.

"Must be Mirza. How well do you know this Mirza?"

"He's just a friend, Mummy."

And there I had to let it go — until he called again.

It was five in the morning and the doves roosting in our air conditioner were just waking when the phone rang. I answered it and there came that man's voice again, "Is Simran there?"

"There is no Simran at this number," I said in my severest teacher's voice.

"No, no, please. Don't hang up," said the voice. "I know she is there. Please let me speak to her."

Veeru was stirring in bed so I said, "You have the wrong number." And I hung up.

"Who was that?" said Veeru sleepily.

"Wrong number." I wrapped my shawl around me and put on my warm slippers. Our house is built for cross-ventilation in the ten months of Delhi summer, and it's draughty and cold in the short winter.

I padded into Simran's room and said, "That man called you again."

She said, "So why didn't you wake me? I would have told him you don't like my getting calls from him and I'm sure he would stop."

"To think I believed you when you said he was just a friend," I said.

"He is — was — just a friend, Mummy!"

I wanted to smack her as if she was five years old. "Are you mad? No man calls an unmarried woman from overseas in the home of her parents if he's just a friend! You must have encouraged him somehow."

She considered this carefully. "No, I don't remember encouraging him. I felt sorry for him, but I didn't feel anything else."

"It's not a question of what you felt, Simran. How do you think it looks?"

"But I'm telling you how it was, Mummy. Isn't that enough?"

I wanted to believe her, but my fear was too strong. I said, "Well, don't let him call again, because I will have to tell your father."

"Don't worry, it costs money to call India all the way from America. He's not a rich fellow, I know. Anyway, next time I will pick up the phone and tell him."

"You will do nothing of the sort."

MIRZA

I wandered around the campus for hours, peering into empty classrooms, turning lights on and off, taking the stairs one at a time, two at a time, three at a time. I went to the Union and sat before the TV eating candy bars and popcorn and trying to laugh when the sitcom audiences did. Even the janitors — sweepers, we call them in Pakistan — looked at me without expression. I went down to the gym thinking exercise would bring sleep, but I found I didn't know how to use the exercise machines, and there were women shamelessly baring their bodies in the swimming pool, so I left.

And from every pay phone I passed, I tried to reach my lost Simran. By this time I was convinced her parents had her engaged, and married off as well. I was in mourning already, imagining her committing suicide on her wedding night rather than marry anyone except her loving Mirza. Then I would become incensed, shouting "I hate her!" across the deserted football field.

I began to read the Koran and feel its truth. "Oh, you who believe, do not take My enemies and your enemies as friends.

You show kindness to them, but they reject the true way that has come to you. They expelled the Prophet and you, for you believe in God your Lord. If you have come out to struggle in My cause, having sought My acceptance, do not be friendly with them in secret."

I told myself I should not have loved her in secret. That was my sin. I should have told her the words every day so that she could not forget, so that she would begin to think about her unbelief and know that I would wish for her to believe, that she might be mine. Every time her mother cut the tenuous connection between us, the more desperate I became to speak with her, just once.

AMRIT

Veeru found out about it, as I knew he would. How many times could I protect her by saying the phone calls at all times of day and night were just more wrong numbers? He had a long, intense, sorrowful talk with her, explaining how much she had disappointed him, describing the dreadful things people would say if they ever found out that she had consorted with a Muslim fellow. Still she denied it, as he explained disgrace as patiently as though she were a visitor from some other country. I felt now she was definitely pretending to be innocent. I even began to worry if she was still a virgin. I would look at her face and think, "America has taught her to lie to her parents."

When the phone calls became more frequent, so that the phone would ring almost as soon as I pressed the hook, we forbade the servants to answer the phone, just as we had forbidden Simran, but they could all feel our discomfort, our suspicions. Kanti watched me from the kitchen, wondering. Always she had been my confidante, my own loyal woman, but this was a family matter and I could not speak of it to her, could not admit my daughter had so betrayed her parents, we — enlightened, well-travelled, English-speaking parents — who had always allowed her as much freedom as if she had been a boy, we who were even willing to spend fifteen thousand dollars on a woman's foreign education. My own father would never have wasted his money in such a fashion.

We concentrated on introducing her to several very well-to-do families, hoping for a quick engagement that would protect her from all men, Muslim or otherwise, but the mothers of well-educated boys were wary.

"Did you live in a co-ed dorm on campus or in a girl's dorm?" they asked.

And she, with a stupidity that made me want to throw out all her fancy books, replied truthfully, "In a co-ed dorm."

Then I would watch them encircle their precious sons with mental shields against my dim-witted daughter.

She seemed to delight in telling them just what she had been studying, although the effect it had was to make them afraid for their sons. Veeru even explained to her, "If you want to get through to the boss in America, don't you have to be nice to the secretary?" But his words were lost on her.

Now she stopped protesting her innocence as much as before and began to sit in her room for hours on end.

"What are you doing?" I would ask.

"Thinking," she would answer.

With her three-week visit drawing to an end and with the phone calls showing no sign of abating, Veeru and I had a difficult decision to make. How could we send her back to America knowing that Muslim fellow was lying in wait for her there? Of course we could not. We did not want her to be ruined.

If I had any remaining doubts about her absolute ingratitude and total disregard for our feelings, she managed to dispel them completely the day we caught her trying to give Kanti a letter to post. It was addressed to that Muslim fellow. She swore it was only to tell him to stop calling her, to go away, but by this time I wanted no more lies.

"Why don't you read it if you don't believe me?" she wept.

I said, "I don't have to read it, you shameless, ungrateful girl. You think I want to read your love letters to a Muslim?"

Veeru said, "That's enough. You are not going back to America. Not now, not ever."

I expected her to be repentant, to beg for forgiveness. But she didn't. She just went into her room, and after a few seconds we heard a quiet click. She had locked the door.

She never used to lock her door before she went to America.

MIRZA

I went to the railway station to meet every train for three days before the new term began. Then I took the bus to her dorm and saw the residence hall manager in Simran's room packing her belongings into cardboard boxes.

"What are you doing?" I asked. How dare she touch Simran's clothing?

"She's not coming back. I have to pack up all this stuff and ship it back to someplace in India. I oughtta get extra pay for this work."

I sat on Simran's bed and looked out her window. They had engaged her to some fat Sardar, maybe someone with a business in London or the Middle East.

Then I smiled at the January sun. She would find a way to contact her Mirza. I just knew it.

Toronto 1984

PIYA

DayTimer, lipstick, briefcase, skirt, slip, pumps — not too over-stated, I'm training bankers today. Power blouse, though — black for authority. Pearls look Canadian, don't they? But I can have ethnic individualism in my earrings. Let's see . . . lucky I have fair skin.

Yes, I know, Bibiji. Airport cab's arriving in a few minutes. If |they send an Indian driver he won't mind waiting a bit, and if he's from our area of India we'll have a nice long talk in Punjabi all the way to Lester Pearson. You heated the milk, Bibiji? I can't drink that — Omigod, with sugar! I keep saying I like it cold. Yes, Canadian way. OK, give it here — don't look like that.

Where's the computer? Yes, I have to carry it. Achcha, on the luggage cart, then. No, it's not that heavy, Bibiji — how you fuss. It's the-top-of-the-line-Compaq. What? Yes, I have my make-up powder packed away.

Haanji, yes, I will be home tonight. Windsor is very close, Bibiji. Tell Bhaiya hello when he comes home from the factory. He'll be asleep by the time I come in. Awright, Saala kahin ka! Bye, Bibiji. Have a good day. Keep busy — talk to Masi on the phone, all right?

BIBIJI

She's not all that young, you know. Twenty-four, she's going to be. Eat your dal, I made it special strength today because the talk is serious. All day at the factory. You must be tired, son. But listen — don't say you've heard me before — this time I'm serious.

I ask you, is it decent for a not-married girl to go travelling all over Canada, computer or no computer, ji? And when her brother is not a nobody on the street but a foreman in Metal Products and Co. Don't tell me it is a small factory. Your masi's son — he's not even a foreman, just a welder. He was never very bright.

Haan, where was I? Your sister, son. Everything till now has been good. First you got us immigration here, she did her classes at the Polytechnic. But now I don't like this too-much freedom. I'm telling you something bad will happen. Now she's talking of buying a car — did she ask you? No. She says, "I need a car — I think I will buy one." And she's gone to the dealers, looking, you know.

Beta, I know they won't allow her to wear salwar kameez in her big company, but now she won't wear it in the evening either. Says it is too much "hassle." I tell you, this is not good and something has to be done.

Are you listening? Eat some baigan. It's your favourite, no? What I am saying, beta, is that it is your duty to find her a proper match. A boy from a good family. But then I was thinking — when do you have the time, all day working. So I think if you write a letter to my brother in India and ask him to find a decent family — Jat Sikh, of course — I am sure he will do the needful. She's got a fair complexion, send a picture.

See, I made kheer. It's your favourite, no? Best basmati rice, I used. Will you promise to write? I know you love your sister . . .

PIYA

Four weeks since I was hired at the accounting firm, but even if it had been four years I doubt if my behaviour would have been forgiven. Company party, yesterday. Open bar, then they planned a sit-down dinner complete with motivational speeches.

Just before dinner, some old fellow with a red face and white hair stands up at the next table and says, "Please stand for a toast to the Queen." I thought I heard wrong. Stand for a toast to whom? The people at my table began to rise to their feet. My boss nudged me — "All rise for a toast to Her Majesty." My face flamed red. I finally understood what they wanted me to do. They wanted me to stand and toast the British Queen, the symbol of the empire my grandfathers fought against for independence, the one whose line had sent my grandfathers to prison.

I would not stand.

Soon the entire room was full of men and women in business suits standing around white-shrouded tables and raising their glasses solemnly, saying, "The Queen." My boss gave me another chance, hissing, "Stand up." But still I sat, staring at my plate. Then they all drank in unison, and I felt everyone in the room watching our table through the bases of their upturned glasses.

My boss sat down first at our table. "What's your problem?" he said.

"I cannot stand for the British Queen."

"She's Canada's Queen." I know when a man is angry.

"Maybe she's your Queen, but she isn't my Queen," I said. I heard the red-faced man at the next table say, "Uncivilized, positively uncivilized."

"Where are you from?" asked my boss.

"Why, India, of course." I was surprised. The guy hired me. Surely he'd read my résumé.

"My Lord," he said. "You're a damn Paki." He looked around

at all the white faces at the table. "I would never have hired you if I had known you were a damn Paki."

I couldn't think of a thing to say. A tightness held my throat. I pushed my chair back, rose to my feet and walked out of the banquet hall to the coat rack. There, with shaking hands, I lifted my coat onto my shoulders. I left the door open so that the freezing Dundas Street air could choke them if there was justice . . .

I drove my new car home. On the radio a blind dark man was singing, "I just called to say I love you . . ." Bibiji met me at the door with sweet hot milk and elaichi and I wore a salwar kameez to dinner.

But today it never happened and the boss was jovial at the coffee machine. "How's our little Paki?" he said. I pretended not to hear and poured myself a styrofoam cup of bitter coffee instead of my usual cup of tea.

BIBIJI

Masi called, son. Are you listening? Masi called, I say. So? So don't you want to know if a good boy has been found? Yes, yes, I know you wrote to my brother, so what if he answered to my sister — are we not all one family? Getting Canadian, all of you. You want to hear or no? Achcha, listen. My brother knows many people — he's found not only one boy but quite a few. He says we should all go back to India and choose a good one. Masi reminded me about our cousin Sohan Singh. He has a travel agency so we have to buy our tickets there, otherwise his father, Sardar Mohan Singh, will never speak to me again. He's a good boy. I met him when he was about seven years old. He will give us a good price. What is this time-off? Oh. So tell your boss you have to get your sister married, he will give time-off; are you not the foreman? And when have you ever taken time-off? That was because you were sick. Tell him two weeks. It is very important.

If you had not had a vasectomy, perhaps he could have found a daughter-in-law for me also — then my duty would be done. Achcha, baba, sorry, baba. I know you said the Congress workers took you to that sterilization camp, but I still can't understand how they were allowed to make an operation before you had the chance to father even one son. Achcha, baba. I don't know anything. I am just an old foolish woman who wants the best for her children. If your father was here I would not have any worries. Who listens to a widow?

PIYA

There's a falling silent in the hallways as I pass. The Chinese South African who works in the next office drops in for a technical discussion on the merits of different IBM clones and I am comforted. And as he is leaving, he says, as if imparting a warning — work hard. I will. I will. For now I am not only myself, but I am all of India and Pakistan and Bangladesh. I am a million and a half people sitting in one small office in Mississauga. I wear a label and will take pride in being a damn Paki.

BIBIJI

Your brother is going to India, daughter. He has told me to tell you we will be going too. Why must he tell you himself? Am I not your mother as well? Typical Canadian, you got a new car, you think you can give answers back patak-patak like a firework. Too much freedom, that's what I told your Bhaiya. A trip to India costs money. Still, he's willing to spend it on you. He's a dutiful boy — not like you, always answering back before anyone can even say, "Howdy Doody." Achcha, daughter, where was I, you made me forget . . .

Haanji, he is willing to spend two thousand dollars more for you and me to fly home. Now two weeks time-off. That is all you have to get. You just started the job, so what. Can a girl work all day and night? Every day you drive here, fly there. Too independent, you're getting. All week you came home late — are you seeing some fellow or what? Don't answer back to your mother.

It's all settled. You will come with us. Bhaiya has said so, and I am asking you to be a good girl and listen to his wishes. If your father was here, he would tell you for me — but what can I do, one poor foolish widow. You have all studied in college how to answer back your elders; I have not. Drink your milk, now. I have made it with my own hands for you and it is getting cold.

PIYA

It's getting cold. Early December frost on my windowpane. We leave tomorrow. We're all packed, and I called the airport taxi and asked for a Punjabi-speaking cab driver for the early morning ride. I told them I needed a leave of absence for two weeks. The boss's eyebrows rose. Personal reasons, I said. The silence was triumphant, but I got the "time-off" like Bibiji says.

Maybe India is just what we all need. Can't sleep. The BBC should be on shortly.

BIBJI

Sat Sri Akal to you too. Let an old woman sleep a little longer. What's the matter? Not the flight? What happened? Who got shot? She got shot? Mrs Indira Gandhi? When? Early morning in Delhi — two hours ago. Who did it? Was it a Hindu — like the one who killed Mahatma Gandhi? What — a Sikh did it? Son, stop it. You must not show happiness — what will people say? Yes, yes, I know, the sterilization. But her sin was greater than a sin against one man, beta. Pride. A widow with pride. She thought even the house of God was her enemy. Cancel the flight, son. Yes. A Brahmin has been killed and every Hindu will be looking for blood.

Tell Sardar Mohan Singh's son, the travel agent, what's his name, we want full refund. We will buy more tickets in exchange, tell him. For my brother, for his wife and their son. Daughter, you will move into your brother's room when they come. Call the airport taxi — the owner's family is also Sikh. They will understand.

You know, daughter . . . that is not a bad family. They are doing well; I saw their son at the Gurdwara. Not a bad-looking fellow. He uses computers too, you know, for his business. I should think he went to college. I will ask his mother next time we meet — they have been here many years, but I think he is still a good boy. Not too much freedom gone to his head. You know, not become too Canadian.

Achcha, no more time for talk. I must say my prayers for all the Sikhs in India.

Lisa

Brenda eased herself out of the light blue Horizon and came around to Jaya's side of the car. "Slam that good, now. It doesn't lock anymore, but no one's going to steal it around here. C'mon, let's go. Move it, move it, pal. Lisa's going to be here at nine."

Jaya adjusted her embroidered chunni and followed Brenda into the hubbub of Hooligan's Bar. She wasn't really slow, just a little afraid. "I've never been to a bar before," she murmured.

"Hey, dude, where ya been?" Whoever she had greeted didn't answer. Brenda was unfazed. "Two Alabama Slammers, Mike."

Mike obliged and Jaya found herself holding a strange-coloured liquid. She took a sip as if it was brandy and Brenda laughed. "It's a shot, kid. You drink it all in one go, see?" Brenda downed hers, and Jaya smiled. "You better not make me drunk," she said, her voice sounding a little prim even to herself.

She looked around and discovered that the only other woman present was Brenda. The men sat on the well-polished bar stools and their voices made a low-grade hum. "Isn't Lisa late?"

"Nah." Brenda dropped her voice. "Hey, Jaya, I got us here early so I could talk to you. See, I need your advice."

"Why, certainly, what is it?"

"Well, see, Lisa's an old pal of mine. We used to work out at

65

Body Stretch together, weightlifting, and then I got the job at the print shop and she went to work for them as an aerobics instructor." She paused.

"I'll take a beer, Mike. Miller Lite."

Mike served her and Jaya noticed he had a shamrock tattooed on his arm. Brenda took a gulp, marshalling her thoughts.

"Well, Lisa met this dude. I mean, he was a real schmuck, see, and I told her, I mean, I knew he was a schmuck — like when we went out and he was always, like, putting her down, see?"

Jaya nodded.

"Well, she'd been talking about gettin' married from the day they met, that's how stupid some women can get, but I figure she's a friend of mine, she'll get schmart once she figures out he's no good for her, see. But now, get this, all of a sudden that no-goodnik throws her over."

"Throws her over?" This was an Americanism Jaya had not heard.

"Says, Forget it, no way babe, or something like that."

"Oh, dear," said Jaya sympathetically. Some men who looked like construction workers had started a dart game at the end of the room. She still wished Lisa would appear as a reinforcement — a tragic young Miss Havisham, perhaps.

Brenda continued. "So anyway, she's all cut up about it, and I figured maybe you could help."

"Me?" said Jaya.

"Yeah, well, see, this guy says he's gotta go away for a while, like two weeks or so. Then Lisa finds out he's going home and he's going to be married to some other woman. And then he tells her he wants her to move out by the time he gets back."

"They were living together?" Jaya's disapproval showed.

"Yeah." Brenda shrugged.

"So?"

"See, he's from India, too, so I figured you'd be able to tell her what's going on with him."

"Oh." Jaya swirled the last of the Alabama Slammer around in the glass.

"Hey, Lisa, get your butt over here. Hey, Mike, this woman needs a beer."

Jaya's dark eyes met Lisa's green ones. Well, no wonder, she thought.

Like some prostitute, Lisa had blonde hair.

Brenda's hatchback was crammed full of Lisa's belongings and Jaya was struggling to close it with a bungee cord.

"Wait'll we have to carry this up four floors," said Lisa.

Brenda was usually a careful driver, but today she was trying to get Lisa to laugh. "Hey, just how many Indians does it take to change a light bulb? None, they don't want it changed." Jaya was quiet.

Lisa said, "You want some Indian cookbooks? I got lots."

"That's OK," said Jaya.

"No, I mean it, I never want to eat Indian food again."

Brenda said, "Hey, you can't get away from Indian food, living with us. Jaya makes it good, real hot curry, see."

Lisa looked out of the window. "Made it every night for two years for him."

Jaya was ironing a salwar kameez when Lisa's wail shook the apartment. She put the iron down carefully and went to the bathroom door.

"What's the matter, Lisa?"

"Son-of-a-bitch. I'm pregnant," said Lisa.

"Oh, dear," said Jaya helplessly. "What are you going to do?"

"I'm going to call that son-of-a-bitch and ask what he plans to do about it."

Jaya said, "I know what he'll say."

Lisa was suddenly cat-still. "What will he say?"

"He'll say to get rid of it."

"The hell I will. I'm anti-abortion."

"Well, he won't be."

"I'm gonna slap that bugger with a paternity suit and he'll be paying child support till he's a hundred." Lisa was getting tearful.

Jaya sighed. "And what are you going to do for eighteen years to support a child? How are you going to work in the next few months — I've never seen a pregnant aerobics instructor."

Lisa said, "I'm calling him."

"My ma says I can move back with her for a while." Lisa dipped a nacho in the salsa and Brenda rolled her eyes.

Jaya looked up from her econometrics book. "I don't understand why you don't do the sensible thing and get rid of it."

Lisa rounded on her, a tigress with an unborn cub. "It's not an it. It's alive."

"And so are cockroaches," said Jaya, "but I don't notice you feeling anything when you kill one. Besides, you're a little late with your morality, since you're the one who lived with him without being married first."

Brenda said, "Hey, I'm not gettin' in the middle of this one."

"I'm moving out of here. She's on his side."

"I'm not on his side, Lisa. It's just you expect too much."

"Oh, yeah? I don't think it's too much to expect a guy to keep his promises, or to support his child."

Brenda flicked the remote to a demolition derby. The crowd roared.

"No, I mean, how do you expect a guy to go against centuries of tradition, years of obedience to his family?"

"Jeez, I thought love had something to do with it."

"Love is an American invention. It has nothing to do with Indian marriages. My mother says it comes after marriage."

"Marriage. I didn't need some guy pronouncing words over us to feel married. I didn't look at another guy while we were going together, did I, Brenda?"

But Brenda was watching a big truck with oversize wheels grinding a small Toyota to scrap.

"Besides, we were real good together," said Lisa wistfully. "He told me he didn't care what people think."

"Well, he seems to care what people in India think," said Jaya.

"I'm filing a paternity suit as soon as its born," said Lisa. "He's gonna get hit where it hurts — in the pocketbook, for child support."

"Does he make good money?" Here she was, defending a countryman again.

"He's self-employed — an importer."

"Woman, you can't assign his wages, then. You'll never collect, you'll end up on welfare." Brenda reached for the salsa. "The bastard," she said.

Brenda chain-smoked and strode up and down the little visitor's lounge like an expectant father. Jaya sat, knees to chin, running her fingers through her hair and wishing she had thought to bring a comb. She wondered where Lisa's mother was — or any of her relatives. A heavy-footed nurse finally came to the door and said, "It's a girl."

"Awright!" said Brenda. "I knew it. I kept telling her ma she shouldna put blue wallpaper in the baby's room! I gotta tell the guys at Hooligan's so they can figure out who won the pool. I didn't. I bet it was a boy just cuz I wanted a girl." Her fingers flew over the pay phone buttons.

Jaya said, "I'm going to get some more coffee."

"Their coffee's lousy. Heck, get me some, too." Then a pause. "Hey, you know what? I'm gonna call that jerk and tell him he's a father."

Jaya stopped.

"Don't tell him it's a girl."

"Why the heck not?"

"Just don't."

Brenda shook her head. "Aw, get the coffee, I gotta be at work in a couple of hours."

She has her mother's green eyes, and her father's brown skin, thought Jaya, as she laid the little girl in the crib. "Mommy's gone to get a job," she cooed. But baby still wasn't happy so Jaya gave her a bottle of warm milk, rocked her for a while, and then laid her on her stomach in the crib. She began a one-handed rhythmic pat on the baby's back till she fell asleep. Just like a pure-Indian baby, thought Jaya. She made herself a cup of tea and sat down with her study notes to wait for Lisa. Soon it would be summer and she would fly back to India, where everyone is careful to marry their own race.

But in the meantime, here was Lisa, waving a county envelope she'd opened climbing up the stairs. "He hasn't paid child support this whole year now, since she was born," she panted. "Not a dime. Not a stinking rupee. I'm going to have to get him back in court."

"Shshshsh. She's asleep," warned Jaya.

"I don't care. She's going to know someday."

"Well, she can't understand it now."

The springs of the couch groaned as Lisa sank into it.

"Man, oh, man. I don't know that I understand it either. What is the guy, a monster? He knows it's his child, he had to take a paternity test. Now I gotta take him to court again. My ma says I oughta give the kid up for adoption. I told her if she talks like that I'm leaving. She says I'm bad news."

Jaya said, "Lisa, it isn't you."

"Yeah, it is. Always was bad news."

Jaya put her arm around her. "You're fighting years and years and years of tradition, Lisa."

"Quit patronizing me." Lisa shrugged off Jaya's touch. "I think that schmuck just didn't have the guts to tell his glorious tradition to go shove. Brenda says you think he would have supported the baby if she'd been a boy."

"I think he would have," Jaya said seriously.

Lisa walked over to the crib and looked in. "Well, his loss, then. Oh, yeah, I got a job telemarketing for the opera. They say I can bring her to work with me."

Jaya smiled. "That's wonderful."

"They said I have a real nice voice. No one ever said that to me before."

"I'm sure the baby thinks so."

"I suppose. Say, you think you can babysit tonight?"

"Ask Brenda. I've got a class to go to."

"See, this Eye-raynian guy asked me out. He says he really likes my hair . . ."

A Pair of Ears

Balvir arrives before dawn, and the double gates at the foot of the driveway are locked. I tell him it was my fault for sleeping so soundly he'd had to wait outside, but he shouts at my mem-sahib instead.

This man I knew as a beardless boy towers over his mother and shouts — though he could be yawning or yelping for all she knows — he shouts, "You knew I was coming and you tried to lock me out of my father's house!"

"You should be more respectful." I come between them. "She is an old woman left without a man to protect her."

This is to shame him, so he will remember he is a man and her youngest son. A son whose duty it is to protect her. But he looks at me as though I am only a pair of ears for his mother.

"Go sit in the kitchen, Amma," he says, but I can see Mem-saab is grateful.

Balvir calls Khansama and tells him to take his suitcase to his father's old room.

I take Mem-saab her silver water glass and her pills and she gives me a message. "Tell him I am not signing any more papers. I already gave him twenty-five percent of this house last time he came."

I think: Balvir and Jai have decided not to wait till my Mem-saab has gone.

"Khansama," I call. "Serve Mem-saab her breakfast." I can't deliver her message; Balvir has locked himself in his father's room. I can hear him inside, unpacking.

"What does he want you to sign?" I ask her.

"He wants me to give *all* of this house to him and to Jai so they don't have to pay taxes when I die."

"What will they do with this house?" I ask. Khansama will need to know — he has four children and a wife in the one-room servant's quarter behind the big house. For myself, I can go back to Jagadri and live with my Leela. Maybe I will even become a Hindu again; sometimes I need more gods than one, and more than ten Gurus for inspiration.

"They will make condos," she says.

"What is condos?"

"Tall buildings," she explains. But I can tell she doesn't quite understand the word either. Mem-saab studied up to class eight before her marriage, which is more than I ever did. At sixteen, the chauthi-lav of the marriage ceremony ringing in her jewelled ears, she came wrapped in red silk to ornament her husband's home. I came later, when I was widowed and she had need of my ears. For thirty rains since — perhaps longer, for there were seasons when the rains deserted us — I've only needed to know the art of massage and the timing that turns flattery to praise.

"And where will we live then?" I ask.

"Balvir says I should live in a smaller house. He says he is becoming concerned about me here . . . such a big house . . . alone . . . with my poor health."

Balvir's "concern" is like a kisan's for a crop of jute — how much can be harvested and how much will it bring? And she is not alone — I and two other servants are here with her, but we are nothing.

She sighs. "Amma, money — the very prospect of money — is changing my sons."

Changing? I can remember Balvir at fifteen, whipping a tonga horse who could go no faster. And his elder brother, Jai, closing his eyes in silence till the job was done. I can remember Balvir at twenty, laughing out loud at a barefoot beggar who dived into a ditch full of slime to escape the swerve of his car. And Jai in the front seat with him, calculating the amount they would need for a police bribe to forget the poor man's life, should it come to that.

"How true, how true," I reply.

A good Amma forgets almost as much as she remembers.

Once, I gave Balvir and Jai all the love my own children needed. I told them the stories my Shiv should have been told, and gave them all the blessings and hopes I could have given to Leela. Leela and I said little to each other when I went home for her wedding. She understands — I get tea in the morning and two meals a day, and but for this work she would have had no dowry.

I must have been a weak Amma; Balvir is an exporter sending scraps of clothing that would barely cover a child to faithless women in abroad. And Jai — instead of becoming a doctor so he could cure the pains that strike his mother every time she climbs the stairs, Jai is an astrologer abroad — divining if the prices of things will go up or down and will we have too much of one thing and not of another. Even his old Amma knows prices go up and there is never too much of anything, only less of all good things, more of all bad things in the age of Kalyug. So much money spent on his education and he cannot even tell me if Shiv will do well and love me when I can no longer give him money. Foolish mothers like me make astrologers rich.

"Where is Balvir now?" Mem-saab asks.

I listen. I can hear Balvir trying on a dead man's silk ties and turbans.

"He is unpacking now," I say to Mem-saab.

"Stand here while I eat." Her order is a plea. Perhaps there are things Balvir cannot say to his mother in the presence of a servant.

When she has finished I call, "Khansama, tell the driver to bring Mem-saab's car."

When the driver has taken her shopping, I wash her heavy silk salwar kameezes and soft widow-white dupattas and I hang them on the second-floor terrace to dry. Then, using as little water as possible, I bathe and wear cotton.

I hear Balvir send Khansama to get him a taxi, and then he is gone.

"The suitcase was heavy," Khansama says in the kitchen.

Khansama forgets sometimes that he is just a servant. He forgets even more often that there can be honour only from serving those who have honour. He has too much desire, too many expectations, like all young men these days.

"How much did he pay you this time?" I ask.

"Full five hundred rupees."

Half a month's pay just for carrying a suitcase? Khansama fans himself with the notes. He's forgotten to wear the topi to his uniform and Mem-saab will find his black hair in the curry tonight. When Sardarji was alive Khansama learned to make dinners like those served in the five-star hotels — rich curries with chicken and mutton swimming in layers of pure butter-ghee. That was only six rains ago, but even then I had become too old to stomach the leftovers. Mem-saab couldn't eat such food either; that's when I started giving food to Khansama.

"Only a fool would accept dirty money."

He examines the notes carefully, holding them up to the sunlight. They are worn in the centre but acceptable; he has no wit to know what I mean.

"He says he will bring his beevi and son and they will move in here, too."

"Here?"

"Where else? You too are becoming deaf," he says.

"There are only two bedrooms upstairs here, where will they live?" The Embassy-walla tenant lives in the five bedrooms on the ground floor below us. If Balvir moves in downstairs, Mem-saab's monthly income will be gone.

"Balvir says he will build more rooms on the terrace," says Khansama. He looks happy; to those who follow him, Balvir can be the smile of Krishna and Ganesh all in one.

"Are you finished?" he asks.

He wants me to let him use the sugar I need for my second cup of tea.

"No." I will not give away any more of Mem-saab's food. Nothing sweet, and no more of her salt than I can help, till I know the price of Khansama's heart.

Mem-saab returns from her shopping without parcels or bags, eyes red and swollen. She stops several times to rest as she climbs the narrow staircase, and I call for Khansama to serve her lunch. I stand by her as she eats and then prepare her bed for her afternoon nap.

When she falls asleep at last, I can go up to the terrace and smoke. Leaning over the latticed concrete, I light the tan leaf of a bidi and blow the smoke out and down to the Embassy-walla's lawn. Mem-saab will smell tamakhu anyway and tell me I must try to be a better Sikh.

I watch from the terrace in case Shiv's round face appears at the iron gates; every few months he comes to pay me respect and I tell him his eyes will roll round like marbles in his head if he spends more years tending machines that copy foreign music cassettes for sale. It takes him three hours each way from Okhla, and food is expensive. Whenever he comes, I give him money and later Mem-saab tells me he uses me and I should make him fend for himself. But Shiv is a good son — he does not shout at his mother like Balvir.

When she wakes from her nap, Balvir is still gone.

"I will give you a massage and you will feel better," I offer.

She allows me to draw the curtains in her room and bring a steel bowl of warmed mustard-seed oil. Sweeping the line of her back with my strong hands, I talk about old times when children lived with their parents, and then parents with loving, caring children. My massages take a long time; anything important should be done slowly.

I help her to be beautiful, even though she is a widow and her ears hear no sound. I bring water for her to wash her face — a face like the milk-tea I made for her children, not deodarwood-brown like my skin in the mirror behind her. She takes black kajal pencils from my hands to make eyebrows, and I tell her how beautiful they look.

Her hair, resting in my palms as I braid it, is the colour of spent fire-coals. My hair is orange-red in the mirror now — I buy one egg a month for myself and I mix its soft bubble yolk with dark henna powder and water that has known the comfort of tea leaves.

Mem-saab goes to the door of her husband's room and feels the padlock, weighing its coldness in her soft hands. She looks over her shoulder at me and there is fear in her eyes.

"Did he say when he would be back?"

"No, Mem-saab."

"Let me know as soon as you hear him arrive."

"Will you have dinner together?" I ask. We can pretend she knows the answer; Khansama will need to know how much food to make.

"Make enough for two," she says.

When I lead Mem-saab out in the evening for her walk, I am her ears on the street.

"Hilloh," I say to the Embassy-walla tenant downstairs, just like Jai calling from abroad on the phone. The Embassy-walla folds his hands strangely, holding them far from his heart. He takes the word as Mem-saab's greeting, and does not realize I mean, Move out of the way, my Mem-saab is coming. If the Embassy-walla forgets to speak Hindi I cannot help her, and they stand for long minutes, smiling.

At Jorbagh market, I keep her from the tooting of the three-wheeled scooter-rickshaws and tell her the prices the fruit-seller asks. When she turns her face away so that she cannot read my lips anymore, it is my signal to tell the fruit-seller that is her rock-bottom price. She takes very little money with her — just a few notes tied in the corner of her dupatta, so that Balvir and Jai will inherit more of their father's wealth. Even so, she always gives me a little to buy an offering of marigold garlands at the Hindu temple and she waits outside in the shade while I ring the bell before Ganesh and ask him to smile upon my distant children. When I emerge, she offers a gentle chide. "Amma, Vaheguru also answers old women's prayers."

Later, when she has put colour on her cheeks and her lips are hibiscus-red, she is ready to receive relatives. Ever since she lost her ears, Sardar and Sardarni Gulab Singh, Sardar and Sardarni Sewa Singh — people her husband helped when a Partition-refugee's application lay between them and the begging bowl — are the only ones who still come to pay her respect.

They touch her feet in greeting; she represents her husband for them. It's been a long time since either Balvir or Jai touched her feet — or mine.

"Amma," they say. It gives them status to call me Amma — old servants are rare these days, only good families have them. Today Khansama's white uniform jacket is crumpled and he wears its Nehru collar insolently unhooked, but Mem-saab does not order him to change it before he wheels in the brass trolley-cart crowned with a wobbling tea cozy. She talks to her relatives in English about his "stealing." As always, she says she will send him and his family back to his village.

She is ashamed to tell her relatives about the lock on her husband's room and the suitcase that says Balvir is staying for as long as it takes to break her again.

I have made sweet white rasgullahs to serve after dinner, but I should have made Balvir eat them before the meal to sweeten his words.

"You are getting so old, you cannot make up your mind about anything," he tells Mem-saab. He remembers to speak slowly, but it is always difficult for her to lip-read men with mustaches and beards.

I leave out the part about being old when I repeat for her — she is younger than I, after all.

Mem-saab gestures for me to offer him more of Khansama's curry.

"Your father told me never to move from this house," she says. "You know, we built it together, selling the jewellery we escaped with during Partition. I can still see him walking with me through these rooms the first time, telling me this house would replace all we had lost. Perhaps you are right that I cannot decide anything, Balvir, but you know . . ." she smiles apologetically, "your father always decided everything for me."

Balvir scrapes the serving spoon around the bowl. He is too old for me to tell him not to be greedy.

"If your business is not doing well, Balvir, I can give you money. What more do you and Jai need?"

As always, she is too mild with her youngest.

Balvir rocks back in his father's chair, taking her measure through half-closed eyes. Then he lets its legs thump to the carpet, and he shifts. A mongrel, kicked away once, will attack afresh. And from behind.

He mouths without sound, so that I too have to lip-read his words, "Today I made arrangements with a construction company. Tomorrow they will begin building two bedrooms on the terrace for Kiran and Manu and myself to move here and live with you."

Mem-saab looks at me; I shake my head as if I have not understood. He repeats it, mouthing clearly so she cannot mistake his words.

She gestures for me to offer him a chapatti.

"Why?" she asks, wary.

Balvir's strong dark hands close around the softness of the chapatti. He tears a small piece from its slack circle. Then another and another. Intent as a counterfeit yogi, he tears every piece smaller and smaller.

"I will take care of you in your old age, Mama," he says.

She reads the words from his lips. They are what she wants to read, and she cannot hear the threat that vibrates in the promise.

Her breath comes faster. "It will be nice to have company. I have felt so alone since your father left us."

White shreds of chapatti grow to a pile before Balvir. The handles of a silver salver I hold out to him feel as though they will burn through my serving cloth. I come level with his eyes. They are the grey-white of peeled lichees, with beetle-back brown stones at their core.

Dinner is over.

I return the salver to the sideboard with a clatter. I think I will give the rasgullahs to Khansama instead.

*

The next morning, Jai calls from abroad. I answer the phone and tell him Mem-saab is well. I say this though she breathed through the night as though a grateful child might emerge in the morning.

I have always had a sleeping mat on the floor in Mem-saab's room, but since the anti-Sikh riots two rains ago, she is afraid she will not hear a mob of Hindus breaking down the gates, so I sleep closer now, on a woollen foot-carpet beside her bed.

In the evening, Sardar and Sardarni Gulab Singh come to the gates and they find them closed, though I have made Mem-saab beautiful and she is waiting upstairs. I hear Khansama tell them Mem-saab went to tea at the Delhi Golf Club with her son, Balvir, and I start down the stairs to correct him.

How nice of him, he's looking after his mother. Such a fine son," I hear Sardar Gulab Singh say. Helpless, I watch his Bajaj scooter putt-putt away, with Sardarni Gulab Singh seated erect and side-saddle behind.

Khansama smiles as he turns from the gate, and I see him look at a new watch on his wrist. Balvir does not like poor relations.

"He's always been a generous boy," Mem-saab says of the wristwatch. "What a misunderstanding. I'll tell Balvir he must phone them to apologize. Put on the TV, Amma — tell me what other mothers and their sons are doing."

I watch Balvir for three days, but he does not call Sardar Gulab Singh to apologize.

The construction men pound above us. The walls on the terrace rise higher and higher.

A fine grey cement dust settles on the furniture and I tell Khansama to dust the painting of Balvir's father above the mantle twice a day. I am still hoping the old man's steady gaze will shame his son and his daughter-in-law, but last night, when Balvir was drunk enough and he thought no one was listening, he raised his glass to his father and said, "What does a widow need with all that money?"

I heard him.

Not once since Kiran and Manu arrived has the family sat at table with my Mem-saab. Khansama has orders to serve Balvir and Kiran morning tea in "their" bedroom. Kiran says she cannot accompany Mem-saab for shopping, because her taste is *so* different. Instead, she orders Mem-saab's car and driver almost every day — to visit her friends, she says. Mem-saab gives the driver money for petrol and tells him to treat Kiran with respect. And she even admonishes me, though gently, as Kiran squeals that I broke all the plastic half-circles in her brassieres when I washed them.

Every day at teatime Balvir tells her they are too busy to sit with her and talk. He's not too busy to talk all day on the phone to Bombay. When the phone bill comes Mem-saab says nothing, but takes a taxi to Grindlays Bank to get the money to pay it. He's not too busy to entertain every evening, buying whisky in cases on his mother's account at the market. Every night Balvir makes Khansama bring them Mem-saab's best crystal and all of them put their feet up on Mem-saab's polished teak tables and her sofas. He and Kiran sit in Mem-saab's drawing room with their raucous white friends — he calls them "buyers" — long after decent people have gone to bed. Once he made a buyer stay two hours longer just because Kiran gave a bad luck sneeze as the man rose to leave.

Mem-saab sits in her bedroom for long hours at a time. Before her are martyr's pictures: of Guru Tegh Bahadur, the Sikh guru executed by Aurangzeb for his defence of the right of all Hindus to worship, and of Bhai Deep Singh, whose tortured bleeding trunk straddles a white steed and who carries his severed head aloft in defiance. Her lips move, soundless, before the martyrs' image. I think even Sikhs sometimes need images to witness their tears.

"Shall I bring oil for your massage?" It is all I have to offer.

"Not today, Amma. My chest is hurting."

When Kiran breaks a glass bangle, Balvir buys her a new gold one, saying, "You mustn't bring bad luck to me by breaking bangles." I begin to notice the disappearance of things familiar. Fine vases have found their way to "their" room, a china rose that Mem-saab brought back from abroad is no longer in the sideboard. A set of silver candlesticks vanishes. A mirror with a golden frame is replaced by a cheap Rajasthani silk painting smelling of the street-hawker's bundle. An ivory miniature departs in gift paper for Kiran's mother.

When I tell Mem-saab, she says it must be Khansama, stealing again. Then she turns her head away so she cannot read my answer.

"Go away, Amma," she says. "I am going to write to Jai."

Once, I rejoiced with Mem-saab when Balvir called from Bombay to tell us he'd had a son. At Manu's naming, I took him in my arms and I showed him proudly through the gates, to my Shiv. I had expected Mem-saab to send me to Bombay so I could massage his baby limbs or feed him gripe water, but Kiran was too modern for that.

Visiting Mem-saab, he fell once — as children do — and I'd swabbed Dettol on his wound. Direct from the bottle, just as I always had for his father and Jai. Kiran confronted me, bottle in hand, scolding that I would kill him with pain, and didn't I know Dettol must be diluted with water? How would I have known — the directions were written on the white label in English. She'd taken Manu from me to sit before the TV.

And here the boy sits as though he'd never moved, just grown, so a sky-blue turban bobs above the sun-bleached gold silk sofa. A strange boy, still beardless, who needs video-boxes from the market to tell him stories of men and women pale as the Embassy-walla downstairs.

He does not rise as she enters her own drawing-room.

"Manu," she says. "Go tell the driver to bring my car."

He shouts, facing her so she reads him, "Amma, tell Driver to bring the car."

Mem-saab says gently, "No, Manu, dear. You go and tell the driver to bring my car. The video can wait."

The boy turns his head, but he does not move.

"You can't order me around. Daddy says you're nobody."

Offspring of a snake! I stand silent with shock.

Mem-saab looks at me, "What . . . what did he say?"

I turn to her and speak the words slowly, just as the boy said them.

She comes around to face Manu. A small hand grips his arm above the elbow.

"I said, go and tell the driver to bring my car. Amma has to prepare to go with me."

The boy shakes off her hand, but he goes.

In the car Mem-saab says, "Amma, we are going to meet a lady-lawyer."

The lady-lawyer has an office in the one-car garage attached to her home. She wears a starched white tie dangling lopsided on a soiled string above the plunge of her sari-blouse neckline. Her skin would spring to the touch, like my Leela's — she seems too young to have read all the maroon books that line the walls of the garage.

The lady-lawyer listens to Mem-saab with weary though gentle respect; too many women must have cried before her. I sit on the floor while they sit in chairs, and I massage Mem-saab's leg through her salwar as she speaks so she will know there is someone who cares.

Mem-saab speaks in Punjabi, as she always does when there are private matters to be said. She ignores my usual signal to lower the strength of her voice and her outrage assaults us, drowning the rattle of the straining air conditioner. I content myself with interjecting a word or two in Hindi occasionally for the lady-lawyer.

Though I am still her ears, Mem-saab has seen much that I — and maybe Balvir, too — had thought she denied.

When Mem-saab has no words left, the lady-lawyer sees Mem-saab's embroidered hanky has turned to a useless wet ball and she offers her own. She tells me to tell her, "Be strong. I will try to help you."

Mem-saab's hand seeks mine and grips it. Her fingers are cold despite the close heat.

Now the lady-lawyer talks directly to Mem-saab. She tries to speak slowly, but I have to repeat her words sometimes for Mem-saab to read them from my lips.

"You say your son now owns twenty-five percent of your house?"

Mem-saab looks at her from beneath her black-pencilled arches, expecting reproach.

"Yes."

"Then, legally, he can occupy the premises."

This is not what she wishes to read, so I have to repeat it.

The lady-lawyer continues, "We can charge that he gained his rights by putting you under duress. And if you wish to stop him from building, we can ask the court to do that."

"Nothing more?" says Mem-saab.

I want to tell the lady-lawyer to make Balvir and Kiran and Manu evaporate like the first monsoon rain on a hot tar road, but

I am just a pair of ears for my Mem-saab, and this is her family matter, and now our triangular exchange has faltered.

Nothing more.

Mem-saab writes a check and signs a vakalatnama appointing the lady-lawyer to begin her mukadma. She leans heavily on my arm as I lead her back to the car.

Mem-saab is lying on her bed. The effort of getting dressed seems to have exhausted her today.

Balvir is angry. Through the keyhole, I see him waving the papers that the lady-lawyer caused to be sent him.

"This is the thanks I get for giving up my business in Bombay, for moving my family to Delhi to live with you. How could three people live in Sardarji's old room? If you didn't want me to build, you should have just told me so."

I have locked Mem-saab's bedroom door and he rages outside.

"I'll never try to help you again, Mama. You just wait and see. I'm going to have to defend this case and *you'll* be the one to be sorry."

"Khansama," I call. "Mem-saab will take breakfast in her room."

Now I see Balvir swallow hard, changing course. "Amma, tell her she has made a mistake, bringing this kind of money-hungry woman into our private business." He means the lady-lawyer.

I mouth his words for her, without sound.

She turns her head away; there is refuge in deafness. Sometimes I think the old custom of burning widows on their husbands' funeral pyres spared widows like my Mem-saab from the dangers of living unprotected.

She is breathing fast and hard again. Time is not on our side of the locked bedroom door.

*

At the court hearing, the lady-lawyer wears a black robe that covers the swirl of her sherbet-pink sari, and her voice, in English, is shrill and indignant for Mem-saab. I sit beside Mem-saab on a chair, though keeping my distance so everyone will know her to be born high on the ladder of Karma.

The judge is called Milord, just like in the Hindi movies we watch on Sundays, but the people in his court are not respectfully absorbed in the proceedings as they are in the films. I think the judge listens more attentively to Balvir's lawyer, a ponderous man with spectacles and plenty of uniformed peons to bring him notes and files.

I count eighteen fans humming on long slender stems, flowers twirled between unseen fingers, cooling the crowd in the high-ceilinged room. Mem-saab is waiting for Balvir to come to her, put his arms around her, say he will really look after her, say he and Kiran will be kind . . . but Balvir's turban never tilts toward her once. No one can churn butter from soured milk.

Afterwards, the lady-lawyer comes to my Mem-saab and takes her hands.

"The judge has decreed there will be a stay order. Status quo."

Mem-saab looks at me but I don't know how to say the English words. She turns back to the lady-lawyer and offers her a slip-pad and pencil so she can write them down.

Mem-saab reads the English writing and draws her eyebrows together. The lady-lawyer writes some more. Mem-saab repeats the words aloud, in Hindi. "He cannot build the rooms but I cannot tell him to go back to Bombay?"

The lady-lawyer nods. "His lawyer said he had no place to live in Bombay. Balvir said you gave him part of your house as a gift to entice him to Delhi — to look after you."

Mem-saab puts the slip-pad back in her purse. She shakes her head slowly. She does not have enough breath today to discuss Balvir's lies.

"What has been gained?" I ask.

"Time," says the lady-lawyer.

She helps my Mem-saab to rise. I follow them out to the car, Mem-saab's pashmina shawl on my forearm. There is some satisfaction in knowing Balvir will have to take a taxi.

Every day, Mem-saab asks if there is a letter from Jai.

"No," I say, "no letter." And since that one call the day after Balvir arrived, no phone call either. Now I am sorry I told him Mem-saab was well.

The Embassy-walla sends Mem-saab a note asking if he may come to tea. She sends me to him with a note saying Yes. I tell Khansama to make cake and jalebis, and by now I know this means Balvir and Kiran will be notified as well.

It takes her most of the morning to dress and prepare; she rests often to ease the pain in her chest. All afternoon, she sits waiting for tea as though the Embassy-walla were one of the relatives who no longer visit.

Khansama wheels in the trolley as usual, but he doesn't leave the room afterwards. He has to report back to Balvir. The Embassy-walla asks for tea without milk. Since he says it in English, I do not tell Mem-saab, and she pours it in his tea anyway. He should repeat himself often, and in Hindi, if he wants me to help him converse.

"As you know," says the Embassy-walla, "my lease is till the end of this month."

Mem-saab bows her elegant head and smiles. His lease has been till the end of each month for four rains now.

"I have been told I will be posted back to Washington after that."

Mem-saab smiles again. "How nice."

She has not understood.

"Posted back to abroad?" I ask.

He looks at me then. "Yes. Tell her I will be posted back to Washington — say, to America — after this month."

I mouth his words to her again. She smiles at him, but this smile is tinged with dread. "I see," she says, quiet.

He accepts a piece of dry sponge cake and declines the jalebis — crisp tubes oozing their red-gold sugar-water. Khansama will give them to his children tonight.

Now who will stop Balvir — or Jai — from putting their belongings or padlocks downstairs? The judge said everything must remain the same, but some changes cannot be decreed away. Four rains ago, Mem-saab could ask her English-speaking sons to place an advertisement in *The Statesman* saying "foreign embassy people desired" so she didn't have to lease to an Indian tenant. It takes a generation to oust Indian tenants, and they can never afford to pay. But now . . . ? Who will listen to Amma if I ask them to write in their English newspaper that Mem-saab doesn't want an Indian for a tenant?

Mem-saab receives a note from the lady-lawyer; she reads it to me and begins to cry. The lady-lawyer says Balvir requested the court to restrain her from renting the downstairs "until a family understanding has been arrived at." The judge has granted his request.

"What will I live on?" she weeps.

I remind her, "You are a rich woman, Mem-saab. You have money at Grindlays."

"But that is family wealth — stridhan — just mine on paper, for my lifetime. I use just a little for my needs, Amma."

I agree she keeps her needs to a minimum. She has always

had a strong sense of duty, my Mem-saab. It is the reason we understand one another. We were taught that widows such as we cannot claim our men's wealth. That our kismet dictates if our men be kind. But these are the days of Kalyug, and her men have forgotten *their* duty to be kind to their mother, or to me, who also raised them.

So I tell her, "Your husband would not want you to live in poverty. That is for women like your Amma, we are accustomed to it. Besides . . ." and here I perform a joker's mock pout like Amitabh Bachhan in the movies, "I don't want to go back to Jagadri just yet."

She manages a smile, and she says in Punjabi so the words sound sweeter, more intimate. "Don't worry, Amma. It is my duty to look after you." I bring my palms together and raise them high to my forehead. I call on all my Gods to bless her, and now she laughs.

This is my role in the movie of her life.

A Krishna-blue night shares his sky with the moon. I wrap them away behind curtains; the deaf must banish all light to find sleep.

The heat coils round us and the fan is stilled by another municipal power cut. Still Mem-saab complains she is cold — so cold. She says a train is roaring through her head but we both know that is impossible. She cannot hear Balvir or Kiran's party laughter or the tumult in her candlelit drawing room. I bring her sleeping pills and shawls and then blankets, but there is no rest, no peace.

At dawn, I bring her a glass of warm lemon juice and honey, as I did for her sons when they had fevers.

She asks for more pills and I bring her the old mithai-tin with its picture of Vaishnudevi, the many-armed, many-weaponed goddess astride a tiger.

When she takes her pills she tears at their plastic wrapping, trying to find the kernel. She looks at them carefully, holding them in her palm, examining their red, pink and white granules in the capsule-skin as though trying to fathom their power. She takes one to her mouth, sets it delicately within the fold of her lower lip.

She turns to me and asks for water, and I offer the silver glass. I watch the kernel pass her throat, then another and another, her head swung upwards, eyes closed as though in prayer. I have never seen her take so many pills, but then she has never been so sick.

When the pills are gone, we wait a moment together.

She hands the silver glass back to me and drops the capsule peels in my upturned hands. Discarded silver foil and plastic with English writing on the back. Letters that sit squat, round and comfortable, unlike our letters that hang from tired arms like rows of ragged kameezes fluttering upon a clothes line. It is my left, my unclean hand, that has learned to make Hindi letters, and so I only make them when I have to write something for Mem-saab.

She lies back and closes her eyes.

"Shall I bring oil for your massage, Mem-saab?"

"Not today, Amma. Stay with me."

I am too old for such sleepless nights; she cannot hear the cracking of my joints as I take my place on the floor on her foot-carpet. I take her soft hand in my calloused ugly ones and I begin to rub gently. "I am with you, Mem-saab, Amma is here. I am with you, na. I am here. Amma is here."

A dying fragrance from the kitchen recalls the turmeric I rubbed on my Leela's arms before I gave her to her husband. She has given me grandchildren, but I cannot recall their faces. Sleep-summoned images dance across my inner eye: Shiv's long lashes — or were those Jai's? Sardarji's haughty gaze, Balvir's eyes downcast before it. Fragments of soft chappati fall from Balvir's hands and shrivel before I can reach them. My tongue seems afire with hot chillies. I cannot speak — and if I speak, who will listen to Amma?

People's voices in my ears. Balvir, shouting, "Amma, tell her . . ." Kiran shrieking I am a fool because I cannot read English. The lady-lawyer: "Be strong. I will try to help you." Manu's voice: "Daddy says you are nobody . . ." Khansama: "You too are becoming deaf . . ."

I am becoming deaf, too.

There is silence. Inert, static silence — a constant silence I thought only Mem-saab had ever known.

I stop massaging. Her arm droops heavy over the curve of the bed. I put my hands to my ears. I shake my head. I hear no sound. There is no sound.

No breath, no sound.

I rise, and the peels of Mem-saab's pills scatter from my lap. I discover I am weeping. I must not weep. Amma, you must not weep!

Ganesh, Krishna, Vishnudevi, Vaheguru, Guru Tegh Bahadur . . . an old woman begs you, give me strength.

I bring her kajal pencils and I draw her eyebrows dark above her eyes. I bring colour for her cheeks and lipstick to make her lips hibiscus-red. I take her hair in my hands, hair the colour of spent fire-coals, and I braid it for her though she is a widow.

When she is beautiful, I cover her face.

Outside her room, the empty drawing room echoes the taunting revelry of the evening past. I go to the kitchen. Khansama must still be sleeping in the servant's quarter; his new wristwatch never brings him too early to work. I take a sharp knife and return to Mem-saab's room.

"Be strong, Mem-saab," I say. There is always the revenge of the powerless.

I cut her wrist slowly, as though I cut my own. I massage her arm from armpit to wrist with deep, powerful strokes of both hands to fill her silver water glass full of blood. She will not need it now.

In the drawing room, I struggle to climb on a low table. I manage to stand, with the glass in my hands.

Then I whirl. Round, with the silver glass aloft, I am a Kathakali dance-girl of twenty. Blood spatters on the gold silk sofa. On crystal. On fine Kashmiri carpets. On white walls, on the raw-silk shimmer of curtains. I bend and I twist in soundless fury, till there is only a little of her blood left in the glass.

Then, suddenly, I am tired.

I slump to my knees. I climb off the table.

At the door to Mem-saab's room, I dip the index finger of my unclean hand in what is left. I squat again. I paint slowly — for this is important — slowly I paint a rangoli design in my Mem-saab's blood on the white chip-marble floor.

The design that says, "Welcome to this house and may you be happy."

Balvir, Kiran and Manu still sleep when I finish.

I wash my hands, using water sparingly from Mem-saab's bathroom till I remember she doesn't need water anymore. And she no longer needs a pair of ears.

Down the stairs to the concrete driveway. I strain at the double gates. They open for me. As I walk through, I picture Balvir and Kiran waking, finding their treasure soiled and cursed. One woman will tell her God and this one — dark, quiet old Amma — will now tell anyone who has ears to hear.

At Jorbagh market, morning ripens from a mango-blush sky. The narrow caverns of shop stalls are still closed, their rippling silver garage doors padlocked to the ground. The only open shop is the one that sells marigold garlands for worshippers to offer at the temple before work, but today I pass it by.

I climb into the back seat of a scooter-rickshaw, shaking its dozing driver. Weary again now, I settle back in my chariot, Arjun returning from battle. The scooter driver stretches and yawns. He takes his time pouring a soothing libation of oil into the tank. Then he winds a scarf about his neck with a flourish like Amitabh Bachhan and steadies the eager bounce of the scooter's green plastic-tasselled handles.

"Where are you going, Amma?" he shouts over the engine.

For a second, I hesitate. Shiv is closer. Then my mind clears; a woman will understand. "To the railway station," I say.

"Luggage?"

"No luggage," I say. Just a pair of ears and a very long memory. Leela will be surprised to see me.

Nothing Must Spoil This Visit

"Watch it!"

Janet winced as the Maruti swerved onto gravel to avoid another overburdened truck. She turned to glare at its driver, but all she could see were the words painted on the back: "Horn Please OK TA TA." In Toronto he'd have been stopped for speeding, not wearing a seat belt, reckless endangerment, driving on the wrong side of the road, you name it.

"Relax," unflappable Arvind said. "Pretend you're on a ride at Canada's Wonderland."

"I'm trying."

"Wait till we get off the GT Road — the climb to Shimla is fabulous. You'll love it."

A rose-silver dawn edged out the dark and Janet peered at the parched barren flatness of the north Indian plain. A slow tickle of sweat began its daily crawl at her temples. Soon, the sun knifed the sky and a fine dust jetted from the car's useless air conditioner and began to settle thick on her contact lenses. She leaned forward and turned it off. Arvind had begun another lesson in Indian history.

"We're passing through Panipat. Three battles were fought on those fields." He pointed, but all she could see were roadside shacks, three-wheeled tempos carrying loads cloaked in jute bags, men on bicycles, always more bicycles. She rolled down the window, unfettering the hot breath of May; it flattened her into the black vinyl.

"Want some sun screen?" She offered him the plastic tube she'd thought to buy at Shoppers Drug Mart; Arvind waved it away as he wove the car between plodding bullock carts and listing, vomit-streaked buses.

India, up close. Ugliness, dirt, poverty, people. Janet closed smarting eyes.

At the white-marbled Indira Gandhi International Airport a week ago, they had been met by Kamal and his wife, Chaya. Janet had expected the brothers to be more demonstrative after ten years apart, but they'd given one another a ritual hug, no more. She'd said to Kamal, "I didn't expect you to be taller than Arvind — he always calls you his little brother."

She hadn't been able to tell if Kamal's reply was sarcastic or just overly formal. "Arvind is shorter only because he no longer wears a turban."

Chaya had sparked to life briefly under that fluorescent glare — and never since. Bedecked and a-jingle with gold bracelets, gold anklets and gold chains for their 4 a.m. arrival, she had first held Arvind close and then scanned Janet with a curiosity that took in her travel-crumpled jeans, clear-plastic-rimmed spectacles and the remnant of a perm in her brown hair.

"She's very fair," she said to Arvind.

"She'll get a tan on this trip!" he replied.

Janet found herself snapping at Arvind, "Come on, let's get going."

Chaya still held Arvind's arm.

They followed Kamal's jeans and kurta and let his glowering intensity cut through the press of the crowds. He hailed a darting brown uniform to carry the luggage, which was full of 220-volt appliances Arvind had bought in Little India, and took custody himself of the duty-free liquor bag, saying to Arvind, "Doctor-sahib still drinks all Papaji's whisky."

Janet could not imagine spry, gallant Papaji ever needing a doctor, but during their week in Delhi she'd realized Doctor-sahib was Mumji's buddy. He dropped in punctually at seven every evening to ask about Mumji's blood pressure and to lean his coconut-oiled head on the back of her crimson velvet sofa, swirling a two-inch Patiala-peg of prohibited pleasure.

Mumji was as youthful and charming and gracious as Janet remembered her from that week in Montreal at their wedding five years ago, petite and perfumed in a starched cotton sari, her hair-netted bun of black hair firm at the nape of her neck, her Nina Ricci sunglasses and a solid silver box of sweet-smelling supari always within reach.

Really, Arvind's family had been welcoming and kind.

At the sandbagged black-and-white-striped blockade at the Punjab border, Arvind wasn't questioned after the AK-47-toting policeman looked at his brown skin and mustache through the driver's window. He didn't volunteer his Canadian passport when Janet's was requested for a check of its special visa for the state of Punjab. The policeman raked her bare legs with a lecherous eye and permitted her, finally, to return to the car. He spoke briefly to Arvind in Hindi.

"What did he say?" Janet asked.

"He said I picked up a mame." He grinned at her.

"Aunty Mame?" Surely the policeman couldn't have seen that film.

"No. A mame is a contraction of mem-sahib."

"Not meant as a polite term, I'm sure."

"It's what they call all white women."

"Why didn't you show him your passport?" Her sense of fairness was offended.

"He didn't ask."

"Why not?"

"He took me for a Hindu, since I no longer wear a turban."

"Why didn't you correct him?"

Arvind slowed for bright orange Escort tractors rainbowed with the turbans of farmers, but he didn't answer.

It wasn't a bit like him and it wasn't fair to her — she wasn't some ignorant tourist who'd read just one guide book; she was a woman who'd learned to make perfect samosas for him from Mrs. Yogi Bhajan's cookbook and who'd studied the art and the history of India.

"Why didn't you correct him?" she repeated.

Arvind still didn't answer.

"Look! Stop, Arvind! There's a pottery stall."

Arvind pulled over and watched Janet bound out of the car, rupees at the ready. Those gaudy Hindu idols weren't the calibre of the artifacts she worked to restore at the Royal Ontario Museum, but they would feed her thirst for the exotic for a while. He checked the car's water level while he waited — what Janet called his engineer's tinkering was all the meditation or prayer he ever needed. Anyu, strange old Hungarian bird, had waited till Janet was ten to break the news about Santa Claus, but she'd never taught Janet to pray.

"Arvind, come see the baskets. Such beautiful baskets."

Janet didn't wait for him anyway. She, who wouldn't trust herself to bargain with a Yonge Street junk dealer, would bargain in broken Hindi for baskets, as if a dollar here or there would make a difference to their life.

She was as excited in India as he'd been when he first arrived in Montreal. He'd met her the month after he'd bought his first Jaguar. She'd read to him from her art history textbooks while he lay, asphalt cool at his back, under the car, and she'd trusted he'd take her someplace beautiful . . . eventually. He'd tried to show her the rhyme and the reason of that Jag's engine, but she couldn't find beauty under all that dirt and grease.

How could he expect her to understand why he hadn't shown the policeman his passport with the visa permitting him to enter his home state, the visa so stamped and official? There she was, aglow in that inviolable cocoon of Canadian niceness. Whereas he and the policeman were like the twigs of those baskets in the stall — woven together, yet tense with a contained rebellion. You couldn't pull one twig from those baskets without unravelling the whole. He couldn't talk about possible danger and unpleasantness if it were obvious he was a Sikh, couldn't remind her about the articles she'd clipped from the paper for him — articles on the massacre of Sikhs at the Golden Temple just two years ago, articles that referred to all Sikhs as terrorists. Honesty may be the best policy when you're faced with a Mountie, but here . . . nothing must spoil this visit.

"How much is pachas rupaya?" The shopkeeper's English vocabulary was proving as limited as Janet's Hindi.

"Fifty," he said. Somewhere between Montreal and Toronto, he'd given up arguing against her belief that people all over the world are the same, just with different languages, art and music. When they'd abandoned his turbans and left long arcs of his brown-black hair on the floor of a Greek barbershop in Montreal, a city become hostile to his English, hadn't she suppressed her French, ignoring Toronto's bilingual road signs? She who spoke Hungarian on her Sunday long-distance phone calls to Anyu now called herself an anglophone.

"Can we fit these in the back seat?" Janet beamed, a basket under each arm.

In Montreal, Janet had been enchanted when he had bent his (then) turbaned head over a sitar, cross-legged on his sole item of furniture, a mattress. It must have been Anyu who'd made her daughter this seeker of beautiful things, past and present. Anyu, who must have taken a vow on arriving in Canada to fashion her Janet's life into a procession of perfect, agreeable, beautiful experiences. Somehow, Anyu had protected her daughter's illusions through the seventies, and now he had the job.

"Move the garment bag, would you?" Janet's triumph was palpable.

But he knew Anyu still warned from Montreal, "Don't have children yet, it may not work out." Janet hadn't told Anyu yet (and neither had he) that it wasn't a matter of choice.

Looking out at earth-tone people blending into earth-tone villages — some with TV antennae rising from thatch — Janet remembered how enthusiastic she'd been about this trip. She wanted to experience India with him, his India, the India he'd told her of so many times. As soon as they'd arrived at his parents' home, Arvind had changed from pants and a jacket and tie to a white kurta-pyjama and sandals. When she'd worn a sari, thinking to please Papaji, the whole family had applauded.

Only Chaya remarked, "She walks so funny in a sari."

It was true, of course. Arvind tried to teach her to glide a little more gracefully, but she'd reverted to pants and a T-shirt the next day.

Mumji, always so charming, had tried to persuade her to return to the unaccustomed garb or at least try a salwar kameez, murmuring, "The best clothes for heat and modesty have been tested over centuries, dear."

Arvind had come to her defence. "Janet comes from a young country, Mumji. Women in Canada believe in learning by experience."

She'd seen Kamal then, looking over at Chaya as though afraid this remark was inappropriate for her ears, but Chaya sat with her vacuous smile, stroking her son's handkerchiefed topknot.

Mumji had coaxed everyone back into harmony with a teasing smile at Arvind.

"Not everything needs to be reinvented, even by engineers." She had gone on to admire the width of Janet's hips, venturing the ever-so-gentle reminder that it was "high time" she provided Arvind's family with grandchildren. Mumji was right — like Arvind, Janet was four years away from forty — but. . . . Now Janet told herself she should expect Mumji's gentle intrusions, and anyway, Mumji was in Delhi, probably fanning herself in the languid dark of her air-conditioned bedroom with one of her *Femina* magazines. Janet imagined herself telling Anyu that her daughter had poured mustard-seed oil on a wood threshold and touched the feet of her husband's mother. Anyu, who had lived under Communists, would say, "You start bowing your head once, it gets easier and easier."

Outside Chandigarh, Arvind stopped at a roadside Government Milk Bar, but Janet was wary of germs in the chilled bottles of sweetened spiced milk. At Kalka, he waded through a throng of indolent men in white kurta-pajamas to get her a bottle of Campa Cola to wash down the dust. She wiped the top of the bottle with a fastidious white tissue and shook her head when he offered to throw it from the car window when she was finished.

The car began to climb the Himalayas. Cooler air released them from the frenetic pulse of the plains. The scent of pine logs mixed with black diesel truck fumes as the little car screeched up winding roads that gripped the mountain "like a python's coils," Arvind said, laughing at her shudder.

He pointed to the precipitous drop to the valley below.

"That drop is called the khud," he said.

"Kud." She could not aspirate the consonant, even after five years of marriage. And anyway, she wasn't planning to use Hindi or Punjabi in Toronto.

At Solan, he stopped to buy beer as though it were a normal adjunct to driving — he even took a swig before getting back in the car. She would not remonstrate. This trip, this pilgrimage, was too important. Nothing must spoil it. Besides, the cool peace of the terraced mountains etched against the afternoon sky, the ebbing of crowds, and the absence of Papaji, Mumji, Doctor-sahib, Kamal and Chaya had lulled her to a dreamy calm. She waved at Tibetan refugee women chiselling stone from the mountain, sleeping babies slung upon their backs, and was rewarded by smiles tinged with slight puzzlement, but never a wave.

Chaya knew Kamal was pretending to be asleep as the morning preparations for Arvind and Janet's leave-taking were conducted in whispers outside the door. She left him alone long after the car had sped away up the next flyover on Ring Road; she wanted this time after Arvind was gone, this unaccustomed silence before any servants began their morning racket in the kitchen and before Papaji's Hindu tenant's wife began ringing her little bells and chanting the daily Aarti, to dream. What if, ten years ago, she had married Arvind instead, as everyone had intended?

It was planned so: Chaya would bring him a heart pure as Shimla snow, brimming with love, and he would take her to Canada, where she would bear many children.

After their engagement, she had grown suddenly shy of the boy Arvind whom she had known all her life. Everyone had permitted — expected — her to give him her love. When he left a month later, she had written him letters in her round, convent-educated hand. "How are you? By the grace of God your Mumji and Papaji and Kamal are well . . ." But Arvind wrote back about the vast number of books in the library at McGill, the underground shopping malls and cars in Montreal, how he'd bought a new hair dryer to dry his long hair, how he burnt two cups of sugar to caramel trying to make parshaad for the Gurdwara . . . as though Chaya had been his younger sister.

Mumji hadn't returned to bed, either, and Chaya could hear her in the bathroom, filling a plastic water bucket for her morning bath. The tap sounded hollow-dry at first, then she heard a sputter, and the thin stream rose in pitch as the water began rising in the bucket. The mame had used two buckets of water yesterday and there had been none left for Chaya to bathe. Today Mumji would "forget" to leave enough water for her to wash her hair. But Chaya told herself she didn't mind; Arvind was gone with his pale, large-boned wife.

She unlocked the doli in the kitchen for the day, taking a mental inventory of the sugar and checking the level of the milk in the covered steel pan on the rack in the shaky old fridge. The cook used too much milk and sugar in his constant cups of tea till there wasn't enough left by evening for Chaya to make yoghurt. Had Mumji noticed Arvind had married a woman who didn't like yoghurt?

She counted the eggs. The dishwasher boy stole at least two a day and Mumji said Chaya just wasn't firm enough. But at least Mumji said it lovingly; her old college friends said there were worse mothers-in-law.

As far back as she could remember, when she and Arvind and Kamal were grubby playmates in Shimla, Mumji and she had recognized one another as Destiny. Mumji had treated her like a daughter, shielding her from Arvind's teasing and making Kamal apologize for pinching her stick-thin arms. When the time came, Mumji had taken a four-man rickshaw up the hill to her father's home. There, over a game of rummy and in sight of the langurs from the monkey temple at Jakhoo, she had personally, though obliquely, asked her father for his motherless daughter, to be married to Arvind. Chaya could still hear her father's belly laugh of triumph — such an honour from a good Khatri Sikh family, with land to inherit besides.

As she entered her son's room to wake him for school, Chaya wondered anew why Janet had denied herself and Arvind children to comfort them for all the things in life that might have been.

A practice chukker before the sun scorches the polo field, thought Kamal. Get rid of this, this . . . anger. He pulled on his breeches and the T-shirt with a Ralph Lauren polo player. Copied in India, but it would maha impress the other players at the Polo Club, anyway. Image — doesn't have to be real. None of the bloody buggers in America who wear forty-five-dollar shirts like this ever lift a polo stick. Image, yar, image. That's all there is.

He put a large brown finger through the brass rings on the boot trees and watched the pale wood slide from the leather. He always felt better around horses, booted and spurred, whip in left hand, mallet in right. A horse must have speed and obedience, and a mallet should be whippy. He took one from the rack in the corner of the room and centred its handle in his palm, testing its spring against the floor. This one was perfect — fifty-two inches. Better take a couple, even for practice; sometimes they broke under the force of his stroke.

Playing polo, he was in control. No one demanded his obedience. He had bought all four horses himself (on his allowance from Papaji). He played pivot on most teams, the player ready to hurtle into the fray to change the direction of the game, unzipping the air with the cut of a backhand or an under-the-neck thwack of bamboo upon bamboo. In the thunder of hooves and the sweating, clashing, knee-to-knee ride-offs he could pretend he was Raja Ranjit Singh and forget he was Kamal.

He heard Chaya in the kitchen and thought he would shout to her to bring him a bottle of cold water. But she would be slow and he was anxious to leave. She was always slow. It really didn't matter — she came from good blood and she had given him a son. What more was there? At least she wasn't like Janet, brash and talkative, asking questions as though she had a right to the answers.

What did Arvind see in Janet? A woman who appeared not to need a man. These foreign women, though, they talk their heads off against male chauvinism, but they really like it, they like surrendering to a real man. Look at their movies — full of gaunt red-lipped women thrusting their come-hither pelvises at every eye. No sweetness, no kindness, no softness. Unbroken fillies.

And Arvind. He was the one who'd had all the advantages. The one who'd removed himself so easily from the responsibilities of love and obedience. Sent abroad to study after acting like an idealist idiot, organizing a protest against Mrs Gandhi's dictatorship . . . now he's a hotshot engineer, come to show off his white wife. What did he want Kamal to do, fall down and admire him? Forget it, yar.

Kamal gave a final tug at the last spiral of his partridge-coloured turban, clumped down the stairs and folded himself into Papaji's Fiat.

Woodville Hotel was cool, gracious and Victorian, but Arvind couldn't wait to walk down the hill the next morning to Knollswood, his grandfather's home. Janet watched him over the rim of a chipped teacup at breakfast in the wainscotted dining room; she hadn't seen him so oblivious to his surroundings since the last time he played the sitar.

"Are we taking the car?" she asked.

"We can't. Only VIP's cars can drive from here to the Cart Road."

Really, Arvind looked quite exotic in his Indian costume — he'd be offended if she called it a costume out loud — but he'd be cold in that thin muslin. She put on her sneakers and a Marks and Spencer sweater over corduroy pants.

He stopped her at the Cart Road above the spur. "Look for the red roof and the apple orchard beside it." The hundred-year-old house sprawled on the knoll with the green-brown khud falling away on one side, but its red roof was peeling and the tin-sheet grey showed through. Between the columns of pines she saw only row upon row of concrete government flats cantilevered between a few sorry apple trees.

They skittered down the steep dirt road, roots of trees offering them natural steps, pine needles crunching underfoot.

"There are the water tanks my grandfather built in the seventies so we would have running water."

Then Knollswood loomed before them, Arvind's days of playing cricket with Kamal but a moment in its memory. This house, he told her, knew solar-topeed Britishers and the mem-sahibs with their white parasols, their corsets and their pallid cheeks. And then the brown-skinned imitations of the British that followed.

Janet said, "Wouldn't it be beautiful if it were remodelled? I can see bay windows in place of those casements, and a driveway in place of the rickshaw circle there."

Arvind shook his head.

"How about a gazebo under that weeping willow," she went on. "And that flowerbed would look wonderful with geraniums."

Arvind walked away into the house, and she was left absorbed in the shushing peace of the Shimla wind in the pines.

For Arvind, this was the house in which he grew up. He half-expected it to be unchanged, with people transfixed like the people of Pompeii, everything just as he left it when he spun westward, slick-reeled in by Promise to a science-fiction continent of chrome, plastic, manicured lawns and vast uncultivated spaces. This was the house he took with him, carrying the worn magic of every room aloft on its Persian carpets. This was the house he reassembled halfway around the world in a Toronto suburb called Scarborough — Rajasthan miniatures, silver-framed photos, Brewer's dictionary, ivory and ebony chess set, Wedgewood dinner plates and all.

Once a Muslim lived at Knollswood — he bought it from the Britisher who saw the end of his Victorian world coming. The Muslim broke a wall so that Knollswood would open towards Mecca; ever since it had been like a woman, with two mouths for entry.

Arvind had told Janet's uncle, a contractor in Scarborough, that he wanted a house with two entrances, and Janet's uncle had said, "A front door and a back door — it is in the plans." But no, Arvind had said, "Build me a house with two front doors, and one must face Mecca, though," he'd hastened to add, "I am not a Muslim." Janet's uncle had given him a Hungarian shrug (shoulders lifted, corners of the mouth pulled downward, eyebrows raised, head shaking).

Once, an amber monkey climbed through the skylight and found a perch atop a jangling chandelier in the main drawing room. Arvind stood in the spot where his grandfather's old cook had stood below the wide-eyed langur, offering his bright blue turban so the jabbering mass could land.

He had bought a chandelier just like that one in an antique shop on Cumberland Street, but it had no memory of any amber monkey.

In the room where the apples used to be brought in from the orchard for sorting by hand, Arvind's charpai still stood — but it sagged slightly.

On the nightstand, a portable oblong with a 45-33-78 lever had played the songs from *My Fair Lady* and *Kati Patang* for hours. Once a parrot alighted on its felt turntable, flipped the switch with a wing and sailed round, bewildered as an immigrant on a new continent.

He was looking for other things in this house, things he might have forgotten to recreate in the Scarborough house, "home," as the realtors would say. He had bought cut-glass vases and Victorian figurines on Bay Street — a lady in a blue bonnet with her tiny fili-greed basket of lavender.

Now that he looked closely, he saw that the one he bought was not as delicate as this one.

In the dining room was the ten-foot table where his grand-father sat at one end, his grandmother at the other, and each taught him different manners: manners for eating English food and manners for eating Indian food. At this table, he and Kamal sat straight-backed with Mumji and Papaji, legs dangling as they listened to tales of India's struggle for independence and their grandfather's hopes for the independent Republic of India. When he was older, the men had gathered for chess every night at this table, often till two in the morning, and neither he nor Papaji nor Kamal ever beat the old man once.

That brass samovar and sink where everyone washed their hands before eating would be impractical; neither he nor Janet would bother polishing all that elegant metal to the mirror shine he remembered.

In the kitchen, there should have been servants who would respond to his imperious shout and there should have been jute sacks of grain in the stone-flagged storeroom. But there was only brown bow-legged Kaluram, the gardener-become-caretaker, who swatted with a rag at spiders in the mildewing cupboards.

In his grandmother's dressing room were the powders and creams of a woman who crimped her hair like Bette Davis and painted her lipstick over her lips to make a Cupid's bow. Checking the dressing table drawer, he found the flaking yellow pages of one of the Georgette Heyer novels she always read in secret, and he hid it away again.

Everyone has things that should remain private.

He stood in the large bathroom remembering when the thunderboxes were taken away and old rickshaw men turned construction workers laid pink and white tile for his grandfather's lavatory, the day the posters from his grandfather's 1972 trip to England were hung on its walls and his grandmother blushed for the shame of those women. And how, after all the expense of installing a shower, the old man ordered a servant to bring in his brass basin and chowki to save water.

Arvind strained, almost believing he could hear the lilting recitation of the Asa di Vaar punctuated by the splash of the two-cup-size garvi rising and falling from the brass basin to his grandfather's body, but it was only the voices of the middle-class multitudes rising from the new government flats in the valley, voices carried to his ears on a gust of mountain wind.

Kaluram doddered up behind him. Loyalty was all this old fellow had to give now and Arvind fell back into feudal superiority, ordering him to bring tea for the mem-sahib.

Janet wandered through drawing rooms curtained in fading raw silk, touching the white cotton dust covers. The bric-a-brac was mostly reproductions, and of the several volumes she examined in the library, not one was a first edition. The huge dark paintings with their ornate gilt frames were copies or prints of European paintings. She began to examine the black and white photographs that dotted the rooms. Arvind's grandfather, young as Arvind was now but carrying himself prouder. Wearing a meticulous turban, a custom-tailored three-piece suit and sporting a cane, he stood behind Arvind's grandmother, seated, slender as a nymph, in a chiffon sari. Other couples, just like them. Serious-faced family poses — Papaji and Mumji, Arvind and Kamal.

And a later one in colour, Arvind looking about twenty-five and Chaya in a sari, smiling up at him, smiling an adoring smile.

This she took with her, footsteps creaking on the wood floors out through the double doors onto the veranda. Kaluram brought them glasses of steaming tan-coloured tea.

Kamal and Papaji began arguing so loudly at breakfast that the cook and the dishwasher boy could hear them in the kitchen and Mumji was becoming distraught. All for nothing, she said, no reason whatsoever.

Chaya came out of the bedroom with a housecoat over her petticoat and an untied sari on her arm. "Please. Mumji will be upset. She cannot stand this fighting."

Kamal rounded on her. "You stay out of this. Go shopping or something."

But Chaya listened anyway, retreating behind the bedroom door. She stored the little bits of themselves that people give away when they are angry; it helped her avoid causing displeasure.

"What will Arvind do with Knollswood? He doesn't even live in India. He's married to a foreign woman." Kamal was almost shouting.

Papaji said, "Beta, that's no way to talk about your elder brother. I think it would give him some interest in coming back to India, that's all."

"Give him some interest! Just give away the largest piece of property we have left. For what? So that some childless mame can live in it long-distance from Toronto? What about my son" — he paused to let the words sink in — "your grandson?"

Papaji sidestepped the last question. "Beta, we did him a great wrong."

"You did. Mumji did. I didn't."

"That's not true. It was your fault." Papaji's fist thudded to the tablecloth; china clinked.

Kamal hissed, "It was an innocent mistake. I pay for it every day." Chaya knew this to be true. He pays for it and she pays for it.

"So does he," said his father, the shame of tainted blood-purity thickening his voice. "He ended up marrying a mame."

Forehead pressed to warm teak, Chaya listened. It is, she thought, a good thing to be an adjustable woman. An innocent motorcycle ride through the Shimla hills and you can end up married to a different man.

They were sitting on the veranda before the rickshaw circle in white cane chairs, barely-sipped tea resting on a cane coffee table, the mountain slope they had descended towering before them.

"You know, you're sitting in my grandfather's chair."

"I am?"

"Yes. He would sit in that chair and tell me how the British Raj brought so many good things to India. Railroads and the telegraph, for instance. We would argue for hours."

"Who won?"

"I did, I suppose. I was raised on history books written by Indians, and I knew all those railroads led nowhere we Indians wanted to go. Later, when he was gone and the arguments lay in the past, I saw educated people agree to dictatorship, censorship and propaganda so the trains he so admired would run on time."

"Aren't you glad you protested then?" She'd told his protest story to women friends at work, basking in their admiration of his heroism.

"It was not enough," he said.

"Enough that you had to leave the country."

"My father had enough money to make it possible. There were others for whom it was not possible."

"Does this house make you want to move back to India?" A question asked in hope of denial; Anyu's voice saying, "This marriage will not work if you have to live in his country."

"Of course it does — but today, there are roadblocks all the way home for us Sikhs. And," he gestured at the remains of the apple orchard, "there's little of our old way of life that I'd want to continue. Can you imagine yourself living here or living with Papaji and all in Delhi?"

Her expression told him no.

"Then I wouldn't be able to move back here." Options that close need no further exploration.

"We could live somewhere." Now she was prepared to be generous, to explore possibilities as long as they would not move into the realm of the probable.

"Not unless we were prepared to live without many things."

"Your family doesn't live without many things," she noted. "Kaluram, on the other hand . . ."

"It's no longer a poor country. It's a country of very rich people and very poor people."

Anyu's voice, "You could never live in India; you are a woman raised in freedom." Freedom to do what, she sometimes wondered. Freedom to satisfy your curiosity if you have any, perhaps. She remembered the photograph and handed it to Arvind. "That's me with Chaya." Arvind examined the photograph, looking at himself as though looking at someone he used to know well.

Janet said, "She doesn't like me, I can tell."

"Chaya? Chaya likes everyone."

"She seems to like you very much." A question, a challenge.

He laid the photograph down before him, a poker player showing his hand.

"We were engaged for a year."

"You've never told me that." She made her voice expressionless. The voice she used at work, discussing exotic peoples' lives, other peoples' exotic history, in other times. Only this was her history, hers and his, and words that should have been said to her years before. Why did she care now, except that Chaya held his arm and smiled only when he was in the room?

"It was not I who engaged us," he said.

Knollswood sighed at her back. Not his choice, so he can't be held responsible. Not his choice. She, Janet, is. She, Janet alone, is.

"Why were you not married to her, then?" Why come halfway around the world to Janet instead?

He cupped the steaming glass in his brown palms. "I really never found out."

"Never found out!"

"No. I assumed she and Kamal fell in love. I was away at McGill at the time and I got a letter from Mumji simply telling me Chaya would be marrying Kamal instead." An engineer's matter-of-fact voice.

"And you never asked why?"

"I thought Kamal should have told me why."

"And he never did?" Now she was indignant for him.

"Never."

"And Chaya? You never asked Chaya?"

"No. They were married by the time I received the letter. And," his hand reached for hers, "I had met you by then."

She was still adjusting to him. A new picture of him. A new picture of Chaya. She stared at the photograph a long, long moment. The pines unfurled and retreated and unfurled again, bucking the familiar pull of the azure sky.

Slowly, with care, she placed her hand in his. Nothing must spoil this visit.

Arvind gave Kaluram a hundred-rupee tip for a daughter's wedding and they made their way back to Woodville. He taught her to climb, lifting her weight from one haunch to the other with the bobbing gait of the leathery-skinned Pahari men who stared at her whiteness as they passed.

"The National Museum of Modern Art? I'll come with you, it wouldn't look nice for you to go alone." Mumji smiled her engaging smile.

Arvind and Janet were back in the furnace of Delhi. There were only a few days left before their return and many relatives to meet. Even the Taj Mahal would have to await their next visit.

Papaji had taken little interest in her thoughts about the trip to Shimla: Did she enjoy it? It was beautiful — mostly beautiful. That's good.

Arvind spent a long time in Papaji's office sanctum the day after they returned to Delhi. That evening, he pulled Janet into their room and closed the door.

"Would you believe it — he wanted to make me a gift of Knollswood." His voice wavered a little; he had been recognized as the eldest son, singled out for a blessing, acknowledged, included. Why had Papaji not spoken to them both together? It probably hadn't occurred to him to acknowledge her presence.

"What did you say?"

Arvind said, "I considered it, of course. And I thanked him."

"And?"

"And I said no."

"Because of me?"

"No — or not only because of you. Many reasons. Large presents carry large price tags. I'd have to fit in here again. I'd have to define achievement as Kamal does, by the extent of Papaji's or Mumji's approval. And going to Knollswood made me realize

Anyu is right, there's no return to the past, so you might as well live where you are.

"I'm relieved, you know."

"I know."

But Janet's relief was short-lived; Papaji assumed it had been Janet's influence that caused his son to reject his munificent gift.

"How is Miss Janet?" he would say at breakfast.

"Fine, thank you," Janet would respond.

"And how is Mr. Hen-Pecked Husband today?"

"Fine." Arvind's matter-of-factness was a match for him. It might even have been funny if Papaji hadn't looked so hurt all the time. Janet decided to ignore it; nothing must spoil this visit.

Kamal avoided everyone as usual. "I have to manage the workmen," he said. "They're repairing the tenants' hot-water hamam."

"I can help," said Arvind the engineer.

"And soil your hands?" said Kamal mockingly.

Not once had Janet managed to talk to Chaya or Mumji alone — always there were people and more people. She had not, she realized, learned to ignore the servants as they did.

Now she had asked to visit the National Museum of Modern Art for the chance to ask Mumji the questions that suspended her in that moment on the veranda at Knollswood. Since Shimla, Janet had watched Chaya closely. Would the Arvind she knew today have been happy with so passive a woman? Never an opinion, never any talk. Spoken at but mostly ignored. Rewarded with jewellery and sweetness for that silent, respectful obedience. And always that beautiful, ephemeral, meaningless smile. Then too, perhaps Arvind would have been different today if he'd married Chaya.

Was it her imagination, or did the rest of the family, especially that drink-guzzling, smiling Doctor-sahib, speak in Punjabi far more than they had when she and Arvind first arrived? Anyu's words about freedom came back — now Janet longed to keep a door closed, to take a walk by herself without company, to touch Arvind spontaneously in public. He was her lifeline to pleasant, clean, safe, perhaps even boring Canada.

At the National Museum of Modern Art, Mumji followed as Janet asked for a plan at the information desk. Five clerks at the desk launched into oral directions and then one of them thought to ask what she would like to see. Janet said she would like to know what artifacts and paintings were on display. The conversation began to circle the domed red sandstone lobby without hope of resolution till Mumji took off her sunglasses and intervened, "Thank you *so* much," she said in Hindi, folding her hands with her usual charm.

"Don't ask them, they don't know *anything*," she said as Janet followed the click of her tiny high heels through the red sandstone archways.

"Then why are they there?"

"They have to be somewhere," Mumji said with serene logic.

They wandered through empty rooms of mostly unlabelled artifacts, and Mumji was a useless tour guide. "Very rare. Thanjavur, I believe." She squinted at a group of paintings.

Janet corrected her automatically. "Gujerat. Eighteenth century."

Mumji frowned. Unaware of any offence, Janet plunged further; air that smells of old secrets should be filtered clean, washed and sanitized.

"How come . . ." she blurted, voice amplified in the high-ceilinged stillness. "How come Chaya married Kamal when she was engaged to Arvind?"

Mumji put on her reading glasses and peered through a glass case for a while. When she answered, her voice did not echo like Janet's. "She had to marry Kamal. He had compromised her reputation."

That matter-of-factness, so like Arvind's.

Janet told herself to be delicate, sensitive to her mother-in-law's culture. "Did they . . . sleep together?"

"I don't know," said Mumji. "Of course he said no."

There were many layers of Mumji's artifice that Janet should have peeled away gently, so gently, but her time in India was running out. "Then what did he *do* to her?"

No answer. Mumji delved into her purse. Janet placed a hand on her arm. No sunglasses, she wanted to see Mumji's eyes.

A look at Janet's set face and Mumji resumed. "After she was engaged to Arvind, she lived with her father, waiting for him to finish his studies in Canada and return. Kamal . . . Kamal took her for a ride on his motorcycle and they went for a picnic alone. . . . I have only myself to blame for permitting it."

"And?" Janet wanted to shout, but that would dismay Mumji further.

Janet could hear the vroom of a motorcycle, with a young Kamal, not a brooding, caged Kamal but a laughing, clowning Kamal lifting a soft-bearded chin to the Shimla wind. And Chaya seated behind him in a salwar kameez, her chunni furling and unfurling like the pines. A Chaya laughing and chattering and dreaming of living with joy.

"And they had a flat tire, he said, somewhere way above Shimla. I believed him, but the damage was done. She had spent the night *alone* with a man she was not promised to, *and it was my younger son.* Now . . ." Mumji was cloaking herself again in fragile gentility, "do you understand?"

"No." Janet wanted more. More. She could see Chaya look at Kamal as the motorcycle choked to a stop. She could imagine them beginning the unchaperoned walk to find a village, down past one precipitous khud, then another. Darkness before them turning the peace of the mountains to malevolence. Narrow roads to be hair-pinned up on one side and descended on the other. Chasms where a woman's reputation could free-fall to ruin.

Mumji continued, "Her father had given her to me for my son and I had betrayed their trust. I had to honour our pledge to take her, but . . ."

Gave her. Took her. As though Chaya were a thing. Janet told herself it was just Mumji's use of English. Oh Lord, now Mumji was in tears . . . how embarrassing.

"I could not give her to Arvind because . . ." Mumji's voice sank as though the pictures on the wall might hear, "because what if Kamal had lied ?"

"Didn't you believe him?" Janet was aghast.

"I believed him, my love believed him. But my duty to Arvind was clear."

"So you wrote to Arvind and told him Chaya would marry Kamal."

"Yes."

"But Chaya loved Arvind, didn't she? I can still feel it."

"Love, shove. I gave her to Kamal and she was protected, not ruined nor cast out. She has been treated well, like a daughter. She has been blessed with a son; what more could she ask for? After all, I chose her because I saw from the start she would be an adjustable woman."

Soon, Mumji recovered her agreeable composure and her sunglasses. Janet followed her in silence through the pale green rooms past somnolent security men.

Mumji asked, her bright, persuasive coaxing brooking no denial, "Wear a sari to please Papaji tonight?"

Janet smiled. It couldn't do any harm. There were only a few days left, and then she would return to her work at the Royal Ontario Museum and resume her contemplation of the exotic at a safe distance.

As they drove past ice cream carts at India Gate, Mumji said, "Please, you mustn't tell Arvind. Don't let anything like this spoil your visit."

*

The stands at the Polo Grounds were almost deserted except for relatives of a few polo players, loyal despite the heat. A bugle sounded the final chukker of the exhibition match and the players lined up for the throw-in. Kamal's team wore blue and gold. "Sikh colours," remarked Arvind. He was impatient today, as though he wanted to be somewhere else.

He would recite poverty statistics tonight, thought Janet. But she wouldn't let him spoil things right now. Because this is it, she thought. This is India. Pageantry and colour. She could say she had been to Arvind's country now, say, His brother plays polo, and watch her women-friends' eyes widen. She brought the camera up to her face.

"You need a telephoto lens," said Arvind. "You'll just get a lot of the field and a few clouds of dust in place of the players."

He was probably right, but she felt a little deflated. Always so realistic. Mirages reflected the players in the distance; they were knights in armour, a few of them turbaned instead of helmeted, but knights in armour nevertheless. A whistle from the umpire and Janet glanced at Arvind.

"Kamal hit the ball in front of a pony's legs in that ride-off," he said. "It'll be a sixty-yard penalty shot."

The players rose in their stirrups at the canter, horses reined in and snorting, as they moved across the field to the opposing team's goal. A helmeted player steadied his horse for the hit. His mallet made a perfect arc, lofting the ball to the mouth of the waiting goal. There was a flurry of hooves, a wild swiping of sticks and the sound of swearing within the mêlée. Then a flag went up, just in time for the call of the bugle.

The hot smell of horse sweat and manure assailed Janet and Arvind as they walked over to Kamal's string. He'd dismounted and his last pony was still heaving, stirrups thrown over the top of the saddle.

"Well played," said Arvind.

"We didn't win." Kamal peeled his shirt over his head and handed it to a waiting groom.

"Get together. Let me take a picture," Janet said.

"Some other time, Janet," said Arvind.

"Let her," said Kamal. "Let her take her pictures and move on."

"Smile," said Janet.

"Just one chota peg and then I must be getting back."

Doctor-sahib smiled his very-wide smile at Mumji, and Chaya rose to offer him the decanter. In her father's home, she was never allowed to pour whisky for men, but times had changed and Doctor-sahib was just like family. He should be, Mumji said daily; he had done so much for them. Still, Chaya couldn't bring herself to touch his sweaty hand; she kept her sari from touching the arm of his safari-suit jacket as she poured the duty-free whisky.

When his glass was replenished, he launched into a story he would rather have told with Arvind present, but Arvind had taken Janet for her never-ending shopping. It was the story of the night he sat with Mumji when Arvind had the mumps and a hundred-and-four-degree temperature.

"I stayed with your Mumji all night. I didn't leave Arvind's bedside once." No one who heard the story ever asked Doctor-sahib what medicines had worked or how his presence had cured Arvind of anything. It was enough that he'd been there, warding off disease with the alphabet talismans he wrote after his name. Even so, Chaya rather liked this story. Now Mumji's soft voice said in her ear, "Get Doctor-sahib some ice, Chaya."

Chaya went to the door to call for ice. When she returned, Doctor-sahib had begun his most favourite story. This wasn't one Chaya liked at all, but one that Doctor-sahib told often.

"Ten years ago your Mumji brought you to me, remember. So beautiful, so sick you were shaking and trembling like a leetle tulsi leaf."

Chaya nodded. Yes, she remembered.

Doctor-sahib wagged a plump finger at her. "It was just after your first wedding night. And you were screaming and shouting and crying like a madwoman."

Mumji shook her head left to right, left to right. "It was so bad we had to wrap her in a blanket so the neighbours wouldn't hear her screaming. If we had still been living in Shimla it wouldn't have been so bad, but here the houses are so close together every vendor in the street could hear her cries."

The cook sent the dishwasher boy in with the ice and Doctor-sahib swirled the honey-coloured bitterness about in his glass. "The monsoon had come so you all had returned to the plains for Kamal's wedding. The afternoon rain was so strong I remember the roads were steaming *pfffft*. The rain made everything green," cloying approval reached out as though threatening to embrace her, "and blessed you and Kamal with fertility."

She moved to sit down next to Mumji. Mumji stroked her arm gently. "My sweet daughter, how you frightened me then. I told Papaji, no matter what the expense, we must take her to Doctor-sahib this minute."

"So there I was in my office just bringing out my instruments for the day, and all of a sudden your Mumji was before me. 'Save my little Chaya!'"

Chaya looked at the floor, her face flushed. Doctor-sahib leaned forward, Mumji's best whisky glass held up to the light.

"I took you into my office and . . ." a dramatic pause, "we had just one little talk and I saved you, because I knew you were a reasonable girl." Now a note of magnanimous triumph. "This whole family was saved from dishonour."

This was Mumji's signal to proffer the decanter. But Doctor-sahib said, No no. He must really be going. At the door, he placed two fingers under Chaya's chin and came close, exuding garlic and his pungent male odour. "Now you see, I was right — everything has turned out for the best."

But Chaya didn't remember any little talk. Chaya only remembered how Doctor-sahib had ripped the blanket from her shoulders and slapped her cheeks, shocking her into a state of whimpering docility.

The way Chaya remembered it, Doctor-sahib had lifted her into a chair and commanded she open the jaws she'd clenched tight since her body had been taken by Kamal. Then he had taken a clamp from the table and, holding her head in the crook of his arm, locked its steel coldness over her tongue.

The way she remembered it, he had stood behind her and twisted her tongue back in her throat until her whole body arched backwards and up and her screams were the terrified screams of a woman betrayed.

And then she remembered his narrowed dark eyes an inch from her own and his so-reasonable voice. "If you bring shame to this family, if your Mumji has to bring you to my office like this one more time, I will tear your tongue out and send it to your father."

And the so-reasonable voice went on, the pain increasing with each word till she thought he had decided to turn threat into action. "Your Mumji is a santini. You understand? A saint! She could have thrown you out when you and Kamal spent the night on that hill above Shimla. But she didn't. She loves you like a daughter — see, she even takes you to the doctor when you have a tantrum. Just remember that."

And then, when there were no screams left in her body, the

merciful loosening of the clamp on her tongue till she could open her streaming eyes.

And later Mumji, entering the room. "Doctor-sahib, will she be all right?"

Doctor-sahib, returning the clamp to the white-clothed table. "Nothing to worry, dear lady. You have a very pretty little daughter-in-law. We just had a nice little talk. She was frightened that she would not be worthy of such a loving family. I told her she should be grateful — she is such a lucky girl, she has such a wonderful mother-in-law, such a handsome husband. I see so many women every day who are not so lucky."

Afterwards, Chaya didn't make a sound for three whole days. Mumji had never needed to take her back to Doctor-sahib's office.

"Where would you like me to put these?" Chaya pointed to a pile of export-reject dresses Janet had bought at the shops on Janpath.

"Oh, shove them in somewhere, I don't care."

Really, Chaya was very little use, not much good at packing and incapable of making the simplest decisions. This woman who so nearly married her husband had a studied ineffectual quality to her incompetence. There were moments when the slight jingle of her jewellery was all that betrayed her presence.

Janet gave up and cleared a space on the bed. "Tell you what. Why don't you sit here and talk to me while I pack. Tell me about yourself."

Chaya sat down, confusion in her face.

"What is there to tell?"

"Tell me about you and Arvind, for instance." There, she had asked it, almost commanded it.

"There is nothing to tell." An automated voice.

"You were engaged to him before, weren't you?" A cross-examining barrister with a reluctant witness.

"Yes. I was engaged to Arvind but Mumji decided I should marry Kamal."

"Did that bother you?" Perhaps a psychiatrist's style might produce results.

"It was Mumji's right."

"But Chaya, what about you? If someone decided such an important matter for me, I would feel terrible. I would feel violated. I would feel angry."

Chaya asked, "What should I have done?"

She was being asked what answer she wanted Chaya to give. Tell her what to say and Chaya would say it. Harmony is the mask that covers the absence of song.

What did she want Chaya to say — that Arvind was her one true love? That she still loved him? Where would that leave Janet? And what right did she, Janet, have to tell Chaya she should be angry about any of the past? Anyu would say, "Anger is useful only when life can be otherwise."

"I'm sorry, Chaya." A weight in her voice.

Chaya nodded.

"I am sorry for you, too," she said.

"Sorry for me?"

"Yes, sorry for you, for you have given Arvind no children." Here lay the true test of womanhood for Chaya, the fulfilment of being, the source, however short in duration, of a pure and devoted love.

"I . . ." Janet began. It would be easy now to retreat into privacy — but her questions had allowed Chaya no such right and she could no longer lay claim to it for herself. She could talk about fulfilment in a life without children, tell Chaya there were other ways to know love, other ways of seeing joy, other ways to satisfy dreams of what might have been, but Chaya would never believe her.

Whenever she'd been confused as a child, Anyu had said, "Perhaps the truth would be a good start," so Janet said now, "It is Arvind who cannot have children."

Chaya gave her an uncomprehending stare.

"He had the mumps when he was a teenager, and now he cannot have children."

Chaya said, "You're lying."

"I'm not lying." Janet was indignant.

Chaya took a long, deep breath. Then she raised her childlike hands over her ears. "I'm not listening anymore. You're a very bad wife to say such terrible things about him."

"Chaya, it's true. Ask Arvind."

Chaya lowered her hands and looked at her sister-in-law. Then she began to rock herself forward and back, forward and back, and soon Janet realized she was laughing. Laughing! Laughing at her? At Arvind? At their pain?

"What is it, Chaya? Why are you laughing?" To be angry at Chaya would be like being angry at a child. She knelt on the floor before Chaya, taking her by the shoulders, shaking her gently.

Chaya stopped rocking. For the first time, Janet saw passion in the flare of her nostrils.

"I'm laughing at all of it. All of it. All of it. At Kamal who was worried about our son's inheritance, at Mumji who wants you to bear Arvind's children. At Papaji, who wanted his eldest son to come back to India. And . . ." dark eyes a few inches from Janet's own, "at myself for wanting all these years a man who could not have given me my child."

Janet drew back.

"Are you saying a man who cannot produce children is not worth marrying?"

"Perhaps," Chaya whispered, "not even worth loving."

Her eyes closed again. The rocking motion began again, this

time from side to side as though Chaya were holding a baby. After a few moments, Chaya's eyes opened and she said, "I laughed at you, too, you know."

"I know. Why?"

"Because," said Chaya, as though pity were a prelude to friendship, "you will have to learn how to be an adjustable woman."

Janet returned to her packing, her movements swift and urgent. Nothing, but nothing, must spoil this visit.

English Lessons

I told Tony — that is what he likes me to call him in America — I told Tony I will take English lessons till my green card comes. Valerie says there are English teachers who will teach me for free, and she will find a good one who will come to the apartment so that I do not have to go outside. Tony says OK, and then he leaves for work at the cardboard factory.

I pick up the breakfast dishes and Suryavir's toys. No one can say his name here — I will tell them at the school to call him Johnny, like Tony's Johnny Walker Whisky.

The phone rings and my heart starts to pound — dharak, dharak. Our answering machine message has Valerie's voice, and I follow the words with her accent.

"We're naat here right naow, but if you leeev a mehsej, weell get right baak to you." But it is only Valerie herself. "Pick up the phone, Kanwaljit. I want to know if you're home so I can drop the kids off for the day."

"Hello," I say. "I am here. You come."

Valerie is a nice person, but you cannot be too careful. Tony says we cannot meet anyone from India till my green card comes, so Valerie is the only one who sees me. I call her Grocery Store

Valerie to myself, because she answered my card in the grocery store, and now I babysit her two strong and unruly boys. What farmers they would have made in Punjab! My son is not so strong. More than two years of women's company. I spoilt him while we were waiting for Tony to get his citizenship, but what was I to do? If I had disciplined him, Tony's parents would have been angry — he is their only grandson.

Valerie's boys don't listen to love or scolding. But they go to school, and Valerie says it is the law, I have to send Suryavir to school. So I went there with her to register him and on the form I wrote the address I had memorized from Valerie's cheques, not ours. Still, Tony was worried in case anyone who might report us saw me. He makes me dress in pants so that I look Mexican, and says it is only a short while now. I hope so.

But first I will learn English. It's not that I don't understand it, but it has too many words. Get it. Put it. I am stuffed. Pick up your stuff. On the other hand. Hand it to you. I learned English in school, passed my matriculation examination, too. We learned whole passages of translation by heart — I had a good memory. Now Tony says I must speak English to pass my immigration interview and to memorize my amnesty story.

A knock. Someone is standing far away from the peephole — why are they doing that? Oh, it's Valerie; she was bending down to tie a shoelace for little Mark.

"Hello, hello. Come in. How-are-you?"

Valerie has found an English teacher who will come to the apartment and teach me for free. But Tony and I are afraid. This English teacher is from India and we did not want to meet any people from India. Valerie said she told the teacher I am Tony's girlfriend and that Suryavir is our son. She said the English teacher was surprised. Indian couples do not usually live together, she told Valerie.

Tony says to tell Valerie we don't need this teacher. But I took her phone number to please Valerie. I may call her just to speak in Punjabi for a while.

I told Valerie I will change my name. I asked her to call me Kelly. No one here can say Kanwaljit. And Kanwaljit is left far away in Amritsar, before the fire.

Some nights I lie next to Tony, here in America where I live like a worm avoiding the sunlight, and I wonder if he knows. And is it only because it was his brother that he does not sense that another man's body has come between us, or is it that he cannot remember the fire we felt in those early days. We only had three weeks in which Suryavir was made. Then he was gone.

If I had been able to return to my parents until he told me to come to America, I would not have been so weak. But to do so would have smelled of disgrace, and I am not shameless. Nor was it a matter of a month or two, Tony told me after six months, when I was becoming big with his son; it would take him two more years.

I tell myself it is not only another man's body that invades our bed, but another woman's too. And yet, that is different. I hear her tearful voice on our answering machine. Her anger follows us from city to city — Fremont, Dallas, Houston, Miami, New York, Chicago — threatening to report us to Immigration. He lived with her for two years, shared her bed, paid her our life savings for a marriage certificate. I will ask the English teacher how to say, "Is not two years of our life enough? Is not my worm exist-ence, my unacknowledged wifehood, enough for you? Enough that I call myself his girlfriend, my son his bastard?"

But she does not have form, no substance in our bed. I can-not imagine him with her black body — and if I can, what of it? Many men pay prostitutes. This one's price was higher and she lasted longer. And he got his green card after two years. Thus am I here.

The other man in bed with us — he has form. He looks like Tony, only younger. And he still laughs at me, waving pictures of Tony with her. Telling me Tony left me for an untouchable, a hubshi. Threatening to tell my parents if I would not open my legs to him.

I did. Rubba-merey, I did.

I thought some force would come upon us then and tear him from my flesh before the act was done. Save me, as the virtue of Dropadi was saved. And it did. Too late for virtue but soon enough for vengeance.

The police came looking for him. Oh, not for my protection — no. They were rounding up all Sikh boys between the ages of fifteen and twenty-five for "questioning." Tony's parent's knew what was in store and they hid him in the servant's quarter, a concrete room on the flat roof of the house.

They told the police he was with Tony in America. That made them angry. One sinewy fellow with a whisky smell took a can of gasoline and slowly, as we watched from the rooms around, and as Suryavir's eyes grew larger, poured it in a steady dribble all round the centre courtyard. They all walked to the door and, almost as an afterthought, the sinewy policeman threw a lit match and the world exploded from silence into horror.

I took no chances. I gave Suryavir to Tony's mother and they climbed out of the back window. His father was blinded by tears and I pushed him after them. Then I ran up the narrow steep staircase to the servant's quarter on the roof.

And I locked it.

And ran back through lung-searing smoke and purifying flame. I was given vengeance, and I took it as my due.

But still he comes between us — the half-dead only half a world away.

*

I called the English teacher today. She speaks Punjabi with a city accent. I will have to ask Tony, but I think it will be, like Americans say, "fine, fine" for her to come and teach me.

Her family on her father's side is from Rajasansi, just outside Amritsar. And she is married to a white guy so she is probably not part of the Gurdwara congregation; they have all heard of Tony's Green-Card Wife. (These matters travel faster than aeroplanes fly between cities.) I will tell Tony I will take English lessons, and that she will be my teacher.

Tony was finishing breakfast when Mrs Keogh, the English teacher, arrived. She knocked and I let her in. Then I asked her to sit down, offered her some tea and listened while she and Tony spoke English.

"Thank you very much. My girlfriend is just new from India. As soon as her green card comes we will be getting married, so till then I think English lessons will help her pass the time."

The English teacher did not remark on "my girlfriend." Good. Not a prying woman. She said, "I am glad to help you and your fiancée."

Tony continued, "I will not like it if you teach her more than I know. But just enough for her to get a good-paying job at Dunkin' Donuts or maybe the Holiday Inn. She will learn quickly, but you must not teach her too many American ideas."

The English teacher smiled at me.

Tomorrow, I will ask her where I can learn how to drive.

The Cat Who Cried

She stood framed by the doorway with the hall lights blazing behind her, grey hair straggling from under her sari palloo, and Prem and I started up in bed, hearts thudding.

"The children?"

"Are you sick?"

"No, no. Worse than that." Maybe my Hindi is fading a little every year; I find it more and more difficult to understand her without her dentures.

"Then what happened?" asked Prem.

"I heard a cat crying outside."

I glanced at the window. Snow gusts swirled over the peaked roofs of the subdivision. Strange how sloping roofs are more familiar to me now than the hot shimmer-haze concrete flatness of an Indian city view.

"Mataji, you must have imagined it," Prem began, but I knew it would do no good.

"It's bad luck. Come, we must do puja. No one will ever say I allowed bad luck to come into this home."

Mataji's life has been dedicated to the collection of strategies to outwit bad luck and Prem knew it, so he stifled a yawn and a

135

groan and led the way down to the drawing room — I mean the living room — collecting little Nikhil and his blanket from Mataji's bed and leaving baby Sheila sleeping.

We had no furniture in the living room, then. Just a large wool dhurrie we've moved to every place we've ever lived since we came to America and cushions of all colours and shapes and sizes. We bought the house because we wanted a crackling fire in the fireplace, but that would have to wait till Mataji returned to India because she'd made it her shrine, filling it with statues of Shiva and Ganesh and Vishnudevi, flowers and garlands, incense and Christmas tinsel. It was her refuge, where she began at five every morning to confide her irritation with twanging nasal syllables, the whiteness of people and the greyness of that twilight that arrived just when she was ready to face another day of strangeness.

"Mommy, what's Mataji doing?" Nikhil asked in English.

"A little puja, darling," I said, as brightly as I could.

"Don't tell him why," whispered Prem.

But I couldn't resist.

"Mataji heard a kitty crying," I said, smiling sweetly at Prem. Then, remembering it's a wife's duty to keep peace, I lied. "So we're going to pray for it."

Prem sat next to Mataji as she began slowly and deliberately to recite the thousand names of Vishnu. Outside, church bells rang to call people to Midnight Mass and Mataji's bad luck cat stayed silent. I wanted to lift myself upwards and follow the sandalwood incense curling out of our chimney.

Mataji was suspicious of me as soon as she heard that her youngest son wanted to marry a woman he had met studying in America. That I am Indian was merely an indication of his good sense. That my parents sent their daughter to study in America was an indication of a family tendency towards wasteful spending. Mataji must have vowed to watch this trait closely for fear it should be passed along any further in her house, for as soon as we were married — in India, with all the appropriate ceremony — she made it clear that I was not to be trusted with money. Within two years, then, we had none left. My dowry distributed to Prem's family — all of whom blessed us enthusiastically — and with Prem unable to find a job where he did not have to give or take bribes to survive, we finally asked his brothers to sponsor us to America.

Mataji has been convinced ever since that I was a bad influence on the son who was to have lived with her in that huge white bungalow on Aurangzeb Road in her old age. When we decided not to have children till we could afford them, Prem began receiving piteous supplications to allow her to know her unborn grandchildren before she died and warnings that he must not be influenced by his over-educated wife. Like his three older brothers, Prem is unlikely to be influenced by anyone, least of all a woman, but he loves being the prize in a contest.

We didn't have children immediately. Instead we savoured the time to be just two of us exploring a new land, freed from obedience to Duty, awed by the power and burden of this thing called Choice, collapsing every night exhausted by endless everyday decisions, decisions, decisions. Prem got a job selling health and life insurance to other expatriate Indians — exiles, he calls them.

Prem is less adaptable than I; he has had much less practice. A few years ago he would have returned to India where there wouldn't be so many choices, but I quickly decided it was time to have children. Mataji came to visit us for the first time when my son Nikhil was born. And ever since, she spends six months of the year visiting each brother in turn.

Usually, she comes to visit in summer to escape the Delhi heat, the loneliness, the power cuts and the water shortages, but this time she arrived in December, wrinkling her nose as she held her sari pleats high over the grey-black slush and yanking her precious bag with its tape recorder and bhajan cassettes out of the dark hands of a helpful old porter. She unpacked quickly and we gave her a glass of sherry in a tumbler that made it look sufficiently medicinal, and then she started her assault on Prem, speaking in English, which she believes makes us pay greater attention.

"I have decided to leave the house on Aurangzeb Road to you when I die," she said.

"Mataji, that is very kind and you can do as you wish, but you know we are four brothers and no one should get more than others."

"No, I have decided. Your father left me this house — that was his gift. I can give it to whom I like. But I have only one condition. You and she," gesturing at me, "have to come and live with me now."

"Mataji, we'll talk about it later. Now you must be tired. Finish your sherry."

Later, in bed, I asked him, "Are you thinking about going back to India?"

"Of course I am. Aren't you?"

"I am happy here," I said gently.

"You can be happy there, too. Lots of people are."

"Lots of people are unhappy, too."

"They are only unhappy if they have no money. We have worked hard for ten years now — maybe it is a good time to go back."

"What will you do back there?"

"I will start my own company."

"You could do that here."

"Not the same thing."

"You want to show your old friends, that's all." My throat constricted. I was afraid I would cry.

"So what is wrong with that?"

"It seems . . . it seems so silly. Just when we've begun doing better. I have friends here, people who listen and talk to me, and you have friends too. We just bought this house and Sheila and Nikhil would never get such attention in school in India and . . . and how will you pay your brothers for their share of the house?"

"Don't be stupid, now. You think I want my daughter to paint her face and have a boyfriend by the time she's twelve and my son to join a gang and bring home some New Age junkie? You just leave these decisions to me."

I rolled over with my back to him. I have learned that when anyone wants to control me, they begin by telling me I am stupid.

I have a degree from Boston University and I know I am not stupid. Of course, being single while I was there and fearful of damaging my reputation at home, I stayed close to the Indian students and didn't mix with many Americans — that was how I met Prem — but I read and read, and I learned how to write my résumé and get a job. Being Prem's secretary these few years, I know something about bookkeeping, so I decided I needed to get a job.

Mataji and I were circling one another like two wrestlers in a ring of invisible spectators, demurely passing one another on the stairway and saying "Pehleh aap, pehleh aap" before each doorway. The politeness was excruciating. We feinted gracefully. She noticed I had placed a statue of Saraswati in Sheila's room and lifted the huge brass piece on her tiny shoulders, saying, "What a silly thing, putting a Saraswati statue in a girl's room. Put this Goddess where she will do some good, in the boy's room. She's the one who will inspire him to learn." I said nothing, but the next day I moved Saraswati back to Sheila's room. I refuse to apologize for wanting my daughter to be educated.

With the tax season beginning, the temporary agency found me an office job in just a few days. I wore pants to the interview rather than a skirt — I've never learned to walk in a skirt anyway — just so Mataji wouldn't suspect anything. And I said nothing to Prem until I got the call from the agency saying I had been accepted. Then I felt weak with daring.

That night I let Mataji do the cooking and we struggled through the burned results with many "vah-vah, bhai vah" exclamations of wonder. Then I said to Prem, firmly and evenly, "I found a job at an accounting office. I have decided to take it. I start next week."

Prem looked at me as if I had hit him.

"Is this how you repay me?" he said finally.

I was silent. Mataji's delight reared its head and oozed around us like a cobra.

"What have I ever denied you?" he asked. He's using lines from old Hindi movies, I thought. And to think I married him because he was an enlightened, educated Indian.

"Nothing," I said out loud. And in my most reasonable voice, the one I use to explain to Nikhil to be gentle with his little sister, I said, "I have just decided I need to get out during the day and allow Mataji to enjoy the children. That's all."

"*You* have decided! Well," he said, throwing down his napkin. "I hope you enjoy being at someone's beck and call all day. How much is this place going to pay you?"

"Eight dollars an hour."

Mataji said, "Beti, he is only thinking of you — going out to work with all those strange men." She placed another burned chapatti before Prem.

"Many women work there," I said faintly. I was losing courage.

But then Prem said, "Well, maybe it will help us to save more money so that we can go back to India sooner." Mataji beamed and I thought furiously, Why don't you tell her I don't want us to go back to India. Why don't you say no now instead of raising her hopes? But I had won this round and I knew when to be quiet.

It was my mother who saved me from disgrace once by teaching me silence. When Mataji gave away a gold necklace that had been my mother's to some cousin whose dowry she was trying to collect, I was so angry that I went home and told her I was never going back. But my mother wiped my tears and said, "Yes, you are going back. And you are going to be silent. No one will ever be able to say that you were raised to be troublesome. Do you want them to say that all your education only made you like some American feminist?"

"How can you say that if you care for me?" I sobbed.

"I say it because I care for you, little one," said my mother. "Here, is it a gold necklace you want? I'll give you another. But you will have to live with the family who has you now."

"I don't want a gold necklace, I want them to be fair. And what is so wrong to be a feminist?"

My mother thought for a while. Then she said, "Be careful when you use that word. Men become afraid. If you want to survive, you must always let a man believe he has you under control. Silence is an excellent instrument, beti. Use it well."

Then she called my old ayah and told her to escort me back to Mataji's home.

But there are limits to silence. I have never liked to discuss money, and I began wondering when I would receive my first paycheque. After four weeks with nothing in the mail, I called the temporary agency and they said, "Oh, didn't you know? Your husband called and told us the account number to which we should send the money, so we've been doing a direct deposit every two weeks."

"Thank you," I said.

That night I asked Prem, when we were in our bedroom and I could hear Mataji's snore droning like a tambura next door, "Why did you call the agency and tell them to send my paycheque to some bank account?"

"Just for convenience." He seemed quite innocent.

"Please, would you let me decide what is convenient for me and not convenient for me." My voice was terse, so he started to tease me as if we were back in college.

"Goodness me, she's getting annoyed."

"Yes, I am annoyed. I would have liked to see a cheque with my name on it."

"Your name on it? Hardly matters, such a small amount."

"What did you do with it?"

"I put it in the savings account."

"Which one?"

"The one for our return to India."

"I thought so." I sat up in bed. "I told you, I don't want to go back to India. Why do you not just tell Mataji that?"

"Because I want to go back."

The snoring had stopped. I felt the room begin to close in on me, and Prem's face became strange and threatening. I tried a deep breath but the air stopped short in my throat. Something else was straining outward as if to rend the seams that held my mask-face in its place, that same mask-face with which I assured friends on visits to India, "No, of course I have not changed," as if change were some terrible catastrophe that had so far been deftly averted. And then the words took form, delicate bubbles blown in the face of a primordial wind.

"Well, then, go back to India alone."

A different silence fell, as if all our years together were but a sleepy musical alaap to this juncture. If our marriage were a raag, this moment would signal tablas to enter the fray to follow the rise and fall of our heartbeats moving in opposite directions. My mother's voice struck up in my head imploring caution, quiet, restraint.

With Prem's gaze piercing my shoulder blades, I put on my slippers and my housecoat — dressing gown, I mean — and went downstairs to the living room.

Mataji's curiosity emanated from her room as I passed, and she soon joined me on the cushions in front of the fireplace. We stared at the expressionless faces of Ganesh and Shiva together, and finally she couldn't stand it anymore. She said, "What happened? Did you hear a cat crying?"

I picked up her little tape recorder, popped in the right cassette, pressed a button and said, "Yes, Mataji. I was the cat who cried."

The thousand names of Vishnu filled the air.

The Insult

I was watching from the living room window as the silver-grey Oldsmobile swooped into the driveway, and, when it spread its wings, out came Uncle Harjit's turquoise turban, Aunty Nimmi in a new lime green sari and their three little boys who can only speak English. I slipped on my spiky red sandals and smudged my kajal just a little to make my eyes look larger and waited in the hallway.

"Aaoji, aao," said my mother as they spilled in.

"Sat Sri Akal, Sat Sri Akal, everyone!" shouted my father as he embraced Uncle Harjit and then, rather stiffly, for the children, "How do you do, hey?"

Aunty Nimmi smells of the dentist's office even on Sunday, I thought, as we embraced.

"My, she's becoming such a grown-up lady," said Uncle Harjit, and he slapped me on the back as he used to when I wore a pony-tail.

When everyone was seated with a bowl of cashews or almonds within easy reach, my father began as usual to describe all the houses for which he currently had listings to Uncle Harjit. My mother and her sister spoke low, so as not to disturb them, and the three boys wandered around the room examining my father's ceremonial dagger collection and staring round-eyed at the tiger-skin on the wall.

"Such a lovely sari," said my mother, although I know she can't abide lime green.

"This? This is so old! I have to go to India soon — I have no clothes left to wear."

My mother seemed about to mention that there are more than ten sari shops on Devon Avenue, but she thought better of it. "Are you planning to go soon?" she asked.

"Next month."

"Will you take the children?"

"Nahinji — they don't like India. They say it's too dirty and has too many people."

My mother managed to smile but I could see she was upset.

"I have never had that problem with my Neelu," she said, speaking of me as if I were absent or deaf. "A very good girl. Now she's getting to be of marriageable age, we will have to look for a good boy."

She wasn't being quite truthful. I was past marriageable age, being close to twenty-three. I felt her waiting. Aunty Nimmi took a few more cashews.

"Girls find their own partners now-days," she said. "Neelu is an American girl — you won't even have to give her a dowry if she finds a fellow here."

My mother sighed. She had asked a favour; she had been refused.

She said, "We have never allowed her to go out with boys. All this dating-shating, kissing-kissing is OK in the movies, but we always wanted a nice boy from a good Sikh family. From back home, you know."

Aunty Nimmi laughed. "There are many nice Sikh boys in Chicago." Again she had missed her cue.

"So many have cut their hair and don't wear a turban," fretted my mother.

"So they make more money, no?"

My mother gave up then. "Shall I make us some tea?"

Aunty Nimmi dusted the salt from her fingers and said, "That would be wonderful."

When they left later that evening my mother said, "She wanted me to ask her straight out, like a beggar. Huh!"

And from then on, she did not speak to Aunty Nimmi.

There were a few compromises. My parents found a "good Sikh fellow" for me to marry in Delhi a few months later, but he had no turban. He'd been driving a jeep home from college on that day in 1984 when every Hindu was licensed to kill a Sikh, and it was lucky for him that they did no more than pull him from that wobbly raft and, with his six yards of saffron billowing on the black potholed road, pull down his knot of sleek, long, curly black hair and take a scissor to it. My father says he must have fought like a tiger as the mob plucked out his beard; I have never asked my husband to tell me why he has no need to shave.

It is easier to live in Chicago without a turban, though, and we were comfortable in an old wood-floored apartment near the El, not too far from the family. But still my mother would not hear of our visiting Uncle Harjit and Aunty Nimmi, even when I said I had a toothache.

"Plenty of other Indian dentists," she said, hunched over the yellow pages.

But very few Sikh dentists. "Singh, Singh, Singh . . . could be a Rajput, too. I'll just have to ask the secretary."

I took the phone from her. "I'm married now, I'll do it," I said.

But I didn't look for dentists. The doctor I chose was a gynecologist, and when I went to see her she said I would have a child.

*

It was a girl, and there were telegrams and letters of sympathy from relatives. "Don't worry. By the Guru's grace, it will be a boy next time." My husband threw the letters from him with surprising force, and he was gentle with the little one, singing her to sleep with a lori and, once in a while, a Simon and Garfunkel song.

A few weeks later, without so much as a call to see if we were home, Uncle Harjit and Aunty Nimmi's Oldsmobile found a parking spot on our street and Aunty Nimmi stood at our door in a magenta sari, saying, Hello, Neelu. My, you're looking pale. Well, girls are always more difficult."

I smiled, "How would you know?"

She didn't hesitate. "Everyone says."

I opened my jar of fine Darjeeling, while Uncle Harjit picked up a rattle and pretended the baby was a dancer monkey. "Tak-a-tak-a-tak. O naach, meri jaan, naach!" The little one started to cry, but my ears were listening for the doorbell or the phone to ring and it would be my mother finding me serving Darjeeling to Aunty Nimmi and, worse, talking with her.

The tea leaves boiled too long before I remembered to add milk, but Aunty Nimmi took its strength without comment, so I knew she had a purpose in coming to see me. It came after a few sips.

"Neelu, I'm very glad you have a child now, because I know you are now able to understand this. Your mother will not talk to me. I do not know what I have done, but did you know I did not get an invitation to your wedding?"

I knew, but I looked as if I didn't.

"Well, I want you to carry a message to her." Then a dramatic pause. "Will you?"

"Certainly."

"Tell her we are thinking about selling our house and, if she will not mind, we would like your father to be the broker."

"I'm sure you could just call Daddy and he would be delighted to list your house, Aunty."

"No, no. If I do that, it will seem as if I have ignored her. Please, take her this message."

She blinked earnestly, and I heard myself say, "All right."

A few minutes later, they were gone, and the baby went back to sleep.

We were hemming chunnis on the balcony, the tall trees of Wilson Avenue dropping the last laser beams of October through the transparent folds of blue and lemon, and I spoke almost as if to the baby in her chair between us.

"Aunty Nimmi came to visit us a few days ago."

"What, she thinks she is welcome?"

"She came to congratulate me about the baby."

"Did she bring a gift?"

"No," I admitted.

"What congratulations, then? Did you not tell her she did not do her duty to find you a husband on that trip to India? And that it is her fault you are married to a man without a turban?"

"No, I didn't, Mummy. It would have been impolite. She gave me a message for you."

Not a movement.

I tried again. "She wants a favour."

"What is it?"

"They are planning to sell their house and so she told me to ask you if Daddy would like to be the sales agent."

"Ask me? Huh." She rolled the chiffon edge tight and looped it over her index finger and I watched the silver needle dance faster and faster in and out.

"Tell her there are plenty of other Indian real-estate brokers in Chicago."

I said, "Are you sure? You won't ask Daddy?"

"Huh. For what? They don't need a larger house. The one they have is twice the size of the one they had in Karolbagh."

She bit off the thread and covered her head with the chunni.

Request and refusal. Honour was satisfied. I knew then that the two-year wound was healed.

I hesitated a little as the envelope slipped through my fingers, and the blue box let out a cold wind whistle. Though it was only November I walked home with my teeth clenched tight so they wouldn't chatter. Would Aunty Nimmi come?

She did. Uncle Harjit brought the baby a stuffed tiger, slapped me on the back and said, "Don't pin this one on the wall!" For once, she hung back, trying to seem unnoticeable in a flame-orange sari.

My mother's shawl brushed past my elbow as she came out of my kitchen. "Aao ji, aao," she said.

Aunty Nimmi grew in stature, and she rushed at my mother and the two sisters held each other fiercely. That was all.

Then my mother led Aunty Nimmi into the spare bedroom we had converted into a prayer room. And when everyone was seated crosslegged on the sheet-covered carpeting before the holy book and it came time to name the baby, my mother said to the Granthi, "Wait, I want Nimmi to do it."

Then Aunty Nimmi rose and sat behind the big old tome with its large friendly writing and she opened it at random and read the Guru's words at the top left-hand corner, so we all knew the baby's name would start like hers, and mine, with an N.

Jassie

I'll be sixty-five this month, and now I know I will die in a foreign land. The nurses are all very cheerful, and my daughter and her husband, who has blue eyes, come to visit me every day. At least, I think they come to visit me. My son-in-law's mother shares my room and there are times when I am not certain.

Elsie is a Christian woman, very frail, very pale. Me, I am brown and my skin is not as wrinkled. She tells me stories from her past but I have none to give her that she could understand. I only smile, and mostly we share silence and the magnolia tree outside. She calls me Jessie, though my name is Jassie, as all my teachers did, and she does not seem to know there is a difference. And in the evenings Ted, the big smiling black man whose talk I do not understand, comes to help us walk down the hall for the usual spiceless dinner.

On Sundays, they have mass on the loudspeaker, and I say the responses with Elsie, out of habit. "The Lord be with you. And also with you. Lift up your hearts. We lift them up to the Lord." But afterwards, I unwrap my old gutka with its handsewn cloth binding and I say the Japji. When I am bitter, I say it loud, as if I do not know the strange sounds bother her. Sometimes she asks me how it is I know the mass so well, and I answer that I went to a Christian school. Perhaps one day when she is forgetful I may tell her some of my story to bring it into words.

We have little in common, Elsie and I. Only that we are both mothers, and our children are married. But motherhood is a word with many meanings.

In those days, many of us had two mothers, and some had more. The more mothers you had, the more rich and powerful your father must be, for each woman — wife or concubine — was expected to be housed and clothed and jewelled. And we, their children, must be schooled in the best of schools — missionary schools, with uniforms and English lessons.

My birth mother was a full wife, married with all the rites of the Anand Karaj ceremony, at sixteen. My other mother was the wife whose failure no one ever mentioned, out of kindness. I was raised to show respect and love for both mothers, and I did so gladly, for both women loved me as their own. This was difficult for white women who had never known the love of children to understand.

Oh, they meant well. I would not have you think that I did not respect my teachers — but they wanted us to follow their ways. I remember most particularly how important was the filling in of forms. "Mother's Name" was written in one box. But for this, I had devised a fair solution. I would give my mothers turns. I had only two, so this was easy.

"Mother's Maiden Name" was more difficult, for our custom was to change a woman's first name to one of her husband's choosing. But the last name of a Sikh woman remains the same, from birth to death — Kaur, meaning princess. I knew the maiden name of my birth mother (it was tattooed midway up her forearm, and she wore a watch with its face turned inward to cover the blue smudge when in the company of Europeans, out of respect for their customs and sensibilities), but I knew not the maiden name of my father's first wife, she being married too young to remember it. So when it came her turn, I would write her married name, Krishnawanti, as her maiden name and hope she would forgive the lie. I would not have anyone believe she had kept a name not of her husband's choosing.

It wasn't as if they did not know and practise our customs, for were they not the several wives of a dead and risen God? And how were they different from the thousand consorts of Krishna, the God of the Hindus? Their senior-most wife was always given most respect; she was called Mother Superior. But my senior mother could not be acknowledged. Oh, it made me angry, then and now.

But I would not say this to Elsie, for I would not have her think I am ungrateful for the teachings of these women. I wondered often if their families had cast them out or if they, realizing their sin of barrenness, had exiled themselves in shame and penance? In later years they told me they chose their exile, but I am not convinced. Widows, even widows of Gods, are not the ones who choose.

In their church on Sundays, with the chants that sounded all the same, burning foreign-smelling incense in the land of incense, they asked us to pray for the health of the Pope and all the bishops and archbishops, although these men were not their husbands. I felt these men were those who had power over my teachers, so I prayed — but not to their God — that they would be generous.

I like to watch the soap operas; they are like the *Ramayan* and the *Mahabharat* — they go on and on. There are some days when I want to be sure there are stories that never end. Elsie likes classical music and says the TV bothers her; it has too much violence.

I say, that is not the kind of violence one should fear. The kind of violence one should fear is always quiet and comes all wrapped up in words like Love until you live with it daily and you value only that which is valuable to the violator.

We were taught to speak like proper British ladies. "No sing-song," said Mother Francis, as we chorused speeches from Shakespeare and poems by Kipling. On the streets our people sang "Bande Mataram" and the truck drivers carried explosives from roadside tea stalls to the Indian National Army. "My Lord, child. Can't you learn to say 'victory,' not 'wictory'?" Mother Mary of Grace said, while in the temples the Brahmins received a family's lifelong savings as prayashchit — penance for having fought the white man's war. At assembly we would sing, "Jesus loves me, this I know, For the Bible tells me so," while the Tagore poem that was to become our national anthem was whispered by poor wretches in prison, "Jana Gana Mana." We learned we should be grateful for the telegraph and the trains and two hundred years of civilizing rule, while Shiva danced the dance of death on trains that carried Muslims one way, Hindus and Sikhs the other. We learned ballroom dancing from Mother Agatha, the red ribbons in our long heavy black braids flying out behind us, while the British packed away their brollies and shipped home rent-free.

Ted says he is not black, he is African-American. And slowly I am beginning to understand him. I have read about Martin Luther King and how he had a dream and then how he was killed, but Ted says his people are still fighting for their rights. I told him it would be easy if the only fight were against a conqueror, against history.

If you believe that everything that ever happened had to happen or you wouldn't be here, then you would believe that ballroom dancing led me to betray my husband before I met him. And then you would know that I deserve my pain and even to die in a foreign land. Mother Agatha said we should have a "social," to practise. And so I met Firoze. Blue-blazered, with his Eton-like school tie, a "proper gentleman," said Mother Agatha approvingly. When she said we came from the same background, she meant we both knew English history and none of our own, that we both expected servants to have darker skin than our own. But this is not enough, even today, with which to arrange a marriage in India. The ballroom dancing stopped when Firoze's family left for Pakistan.

The man my father chose for me instead was a good man, slight of build, quiet and kind. He was the son of Sikh landowners, had a missionary education but no connections. I thought he had no business sense, either, when he opened a shop to sell khadi cloth. I told him no one would buy cloth made in India; everyone wanted cloth made on machines in Manchester. But he believed Gandhi had been his best salesman, and he was right. Every newly elected Indian politician came to our shop to buy khadi.

My father gave my husband a house in old Delhi as my dowry, and my husband gave me first this daughter for my old age and then two sons. I named my daughter with a Muslim name, Yasmeen, in memory of Firoze. Yasmeen Kaur. My Sikh family blushed for me and ever after called her Minni.

Minni comes to visit and she has brought me gulabjamuns, those big, fat, perfectly rounded light brown sweets. But my arthritis is so painful today I cannot hold them in my hands, and she has to feed me as I used to feed her. Her husband stands at his mother's bed and jokes how he will take us both dancing next weekend.

I feel pain just to think of it and Elsie smiles faintly. He reminds me of a movie star, big, white and unafraid. Minni is small and quick and dark next to him and her voice reminds me of Mother Ursula's clipped English tones. My husband, thinking to please me, sent her to England to study, but now I am irritated when I realize it is her accent my son-in-law finds *so* attractive.

Elsie was married many years but she talks very little about her husband. She says he was a policeman and she worried every day of their marriage that he would be killed. I didn't worry about my husband, only about my sons. They were both in the army when the second war with Pakistan broke out. They were the first to be sent to the front, perhaps because they were Sikhs and not Hindus. I wonder sometimes if they fought Firoze's sons.

It doesn't matter now; they are both gone.

After we had given two sons, we sold the khadi store and came away as far as we could fly. Minni welcomed us both, as a dutiful daughter should. But it is cold in America. A coldness of the soul that my husband never became accustomed to. I was cold to him, too — I had never been otherwise. My warmth was left in India, where I earned this pain ballroom dancing to the convent's Steinway with Firoze.

Despite my son-in-law's joking, Elsie is not going dancing next weekend. In fact, I had to strain to hear her breathing last night. Ted came in and helped the nurse to put an oxygen mask over her face, but it hurts her and she tries to do without it. I am able to sit up today and her voice is very faint. "Jessie, will you sit next to me? I think I am having an anxiety attack." I have to manoeuvre my walker over to her side of the room and then lower myself into the chair next to her bed. She is "perspiring profusely," as Mother Conrad would have put it.

"I'm glad you're here, Jessie," she says.

And then, very faintly, she says, "Jessie, will you pray with me?"

I want to say, "My name is Jassie, not Jessie. You would not understand my prayers, and you don't like to hear me speak Punjabi, and you need Christian prayers, not mine."

But this is not the time and she is not the women to whom I want to say the words. I take her rosary from the bedpost and say, "Our Father, who art in Heaven . . ."

I wonder, could I have learned the namaaz as easily as I learned the rosary?

Devika

Soon it would be June. Even so, Devika pulled a shawl close and cradled a fourth cup of steaming tea against cold palms. She had spent the morning cooking mattar-panneer and almond chicken curry and then cleaned everything with the cleaning solution she could just spray and wipe away. She washed her waist-length hair and bathed when the clock told her Ratan would be getting off work, ironed a fresh melon-coloured silk salwar kameez and polished her silver anklets so she knew every chink shone as she moved.

This is what good wives do.

Carefully, she inserted a cassette of Hindi songs from old movies in his new stereo system; his older sisters said Baba loved Kishore Kumar's hits. She wished they would call him Ratan instead of Baba, but all three treated him as though he were still some long-delayed reward for their parents' years of prayers and fasting.

It would be 45°, maybe 46°C in Delhi now and the cyclamen bougainvillea would be in valiant bloom around her parents' veranda. It must be sunrise; her mother would be bowed in puja, chanting the aarti. Maybe the sun had already risen at home — it rises so early in summer — and then street vendors would be crying their wares with dust-parched throats, stripping tar off sun-baked streets with their worn cycle tires. There, scooter rickshaw drivers would be squinting into sun-mirages. But here, on the twenty-first floor overlooking the Don Valley Parkway, the *Toronto Star* sat on the coffee table and, unaware of clashing adjectives, proclaimed it a sunny and cold day.

She unfolded a featherlight blue aerogramme with handwriting crammed corner to corner. Asha — wilful, fun-loving, irreverent Asha, the one who'd sworn never to be married — was transformed by marriage, had a son and now sounded like all the other girls from their college. "Seven pounds, two ounces. Of course, I had all the tests so we knew it was going to be a boy. My mom-in-law was so glad, she even arranged a suite for me in the hospital. And she sent the servant home and slept outside my room on the couch. Devika, this labour is the most terrible thing. No one tells you how bad it is. My mom-in-law paid a lady-doctor from England to give me training so that I would have a healthy boy. The lady-doctor told me how to breathe and to push but when I was actually on the table I didn't remember anything she told me. All that money went to waste. But many people gave my mom-in-law shagan to welcome the boy. Your Daddy came and gave 501 rupees. You know he's very proud to have a daughter married to someone settled in Canada, and a big stockbroker, at that."

Someone else must have written that letter, not Asha. Not Asha, with her "I'll never be happy being married to some rich fellow and having babies and servants to look after them." Not the Asha she remembered saying, "I'd never let anyone do a test on me — I'd *like* a little girl." The Asha she had known had sworn with schoolgirl sincerity to shun the rewards of complicity. That Asha could never have become this woman. Why, everyone in college had thought Asha would some day scandalize Delhi with a love-marriage, be an activist or a lawyer, an engineer, an architect, a mathematician . . . a pioneer . . .

There was nothing more Devika could straighten in the living room, so she took the teacup and went into the master bedroom.

The bed was too large for this room, but sharing a smaller one with a stranger would have been difficult for both of them. That first moment at the airport, she had not recognized him. Husband or not, a year waiting for a visa is a long time. And the few days she had seen him in Delhi were marriage days and one mercifully brief night of pain. She remembered circling above Toronto, with the double-oval letting her see small white planes nuzzling at the terminal below, and the moment of numb panic as the plane landed. Reaching into her carry-on bag, she'd drawn out two photograph albums, proof of her marriage for the phalanx of immigration officials she knew awaited her. And afterwards she pushed her luggage on a cart and walked past crowds of white, black, yellow and brown faces, including his, until he called her name.

Then as now, the apartment had bare white walls in the living room, two bedrooms, a couch and coffee table, a smoked glass and brass dining table with four beige-upholstered chrome-plated chairs, a small bed in the second bedroom — and this bed he told her was "king-size." Ratan watched her unpack suitcases more than half-full of gifts for him from his family. A jar of sweet mango pickles, a plastic bottle full of honey from a relative's farm, two kilos of square-granuled almost-white sugar, two kilos of basmati rice, and a large black metal Nataraj Shiva, which his mother packed using Devika's gold-bordered wedding saris as cushioning. She was confused when he said, "Mum shouldn't have bothered — you can get everything on Gerrard Street right here." Was that any way to treat the love of a woman who considered herself barren till his birth?

That first day, he had let her sleep alone on the king-size bed till her day was more attuned to his. In the evening, they set off in his new Ford Tempo with the automatic shoulder straps that startled her by whirring forward when the doors opened, to visit his sisters and their families in Malton, in Brampton, and in Mississauga. He had asked which sister she wanted to visit first. She had said, "Whatever suits you." "You choose," he urged, so she felt sure she was being tested. She named the eldest, "Vandana Di — it would show respect."

"True," he said, expectation fulfilled. She let her eyes drift to his face without turning her head so she could judge if he was pleased or not, but it was too early for her to read him.

That was her specialty. To read others and to know what they expected. Then to do her best to satisfy, to choose as they would have her choose. "Such a sweet girl, such a good girl," Asha's mother used to say, touching her cheek with a wistful glance at her own daughter. Asha would toss her bobbed head and say, "Don't you mean docile, mama?" The reply would come certain as a Brahmin's incantation, "Docile girls are good, Asha." And good girls are docile.

Ratan asked if she wanted to visit Niagara Falls, although there were no relatives there. Devika had never thought of travel except to visit relatives, seeing the occasional car trip out of Delhi as a test of endurance, a sacrifice offered to Duty. She had always agreed with her mother that it seemed appropriate that the Hindustani word for journey, safar, sounded like the English suffer.

A square of blue window balanced on the bedposts and she leaned close against the pane. A precise ant-stream flowed below and the drivers in their cars seemed to know just where they wanted to be, just where they wanted to go. It was seven o'clock, and still no sign of Ratan. Perhaps he went to visit one of his sisters.

She had first met Ratan's sisters when all three — with husbands and children — flew back to India for their wedding. They had been guests of honour decked in wedding finery, guarantors of certain prosperity for the groom, introduced to all her father's friends as "Devika's Canadian sisters-in-law." She knew her father had no idea Vandana Di made her husband help with the children and the dishes. Or that Kavali Di's daughter worked as a model for a lingerie catalogue. In Canada, she found it more difficult to sort the good girls from the bad ones. It is important to have both, because if there are no bad girls, how would anyone know that girls like Devika are good? Would her mother like her youngest sister-in-law, Bindiya Di, whose passion for butter chicken and kofta curry had imprisoned her, bat-like in her caftans, before a daily stack of rented Indian movies? They were Ratan's family, she reminded herself, and she was duty-bound to love them.

Grey monoliths thrust deep into a tender mauve sky. Along them hung broken chains of light, and Devika realized it was now almost eight o'clock. She went into the kitchen, stirred the mattar-panneer and wondered if she dared call Ratan at work. Could he have had an accident? Quickly through the living room to the balcony. But there was no break in the necklace of twin-diamonded cars glowing on the collarbone of the Don Valley. Terror hit her low in the stomach; she could see no people in other apartments, there were no people walking along the side of the road, no people sitting on the scraps of green between the expressways. No people. A country with more acres of land than people.

What, thought Devika, would she do if Ratan died?

Ratan's hands were light on the wheel. His left foot tapped a disco rhythm to the Hindi film song filling the car. A good day, really, a good day. Peter Kendall, the grey-haired vice-president, had noticed him. After three years on the job, Peter Kendall had invited him to join a few of the brokers at a pub for beer after work. He'd said "awesome" at least five times and laughed into the Molson beer at all the jokes. He hadn't mentioned that Peter Kendall had never invited him before. He'd been quiet in all the right places, especially when the talk moved to "foreigners getting jobs in Canadian companies, eh?" He hadn't responded when someone wondered "why those immigrants don't leave their battles at home." And he just might be invited again — unless he made Peter Kendall mad.

In Indian English, mad means crazy. In Canadian English, it just means angry, but when Peter Kendall got mad Ratan couldn't tell the difference. One time, he thought Peter Kendall would have a fit explaining the need for the Canada–US free trade agreement to Ratan, and just a week ago Mr. Kendall had asked him to sit at another table in the employees' lounge because he said the smell of the curry Devika packed for Ratan's lunch was enough to make him sick.

So today was progress. And, thinking of progress, Devika seemed to be making fine progress. She had settled in and was keeping house as if she'd lived here all her life, instead of just two months. It would take her a few tries to pass her driver's test — after all, it had taken him two tries, even with his brother-in-laws' guidance, as he learned how to drive on the right. His parents had chosen well for him. Now his mother's description of Devika as a convent-educated, "homely" girl made him smile. In Indian English, homely means domestic. In Canadian English, homely means ugly. Devika was far from ugly. Her face was too round to be considered beautiful in Canada, but quite attractive. She had a good figure, maybe a little plump for Canada, but passable . . . desirable.

Maybe she could make a few changes, though. Her clothes,

for instance. She looked like one of those Indian women who promenade on Gerrard Street on Sunday evenings, teetering in their high-heeled sandals on the slushy sidewalks, examining racks of ready-made salwar kameezes from India and gossiping about the Hindi film stars. Whereas he . . . he was moving up in life now. He tried to imagine Devika in a black velvet skirt and a white silk jacquard blouse, like Peter Kendall's wife.

He thought he should reciprocate Peter Kendall's hospitality. Now that Devika was here, he could invite him and Mrs. Kendall to dinner. The apartment looked quite nice with the new couch and coffee table he'd bought from one of the furniture dealers on Kennedy Street. They would have to buy drapes and a better dinner set — English china, if possible — and a set of larger serving bowls, he thought. But the evening would be an investment in his future.

As he pressed the remote door-opener to enter the dark cave of the underground garage, he decided Devika must wear a dress. And pantyhose, and no nose ring.

It was ten o'clock when Devika heard Ratan's key in the door of the apartment. She uncoiled her body from its fear-knotted ball on the couch to greet him as he set his briefcase down and picked up the *Star*.

"I went out for a drink with the guys at work," he said.

"Mmmhmm." She started the Kishore Kumar tape over again. The chicken curry was falling off the bone, but she was so relieved that he was not dead and she left alone in a strange country that she didn't care. The fear still followed her like a shadow as he talked at her through the swinging doors to the narrow kitchen.

"Pete asked me to attend."

"Pete?"

"Peter Kendall."

He'd told her about Peter Kendall before, but he'd never called him Pete.

"You must be hungry," she said.

"Use napkins under the hot dishes, Devika," he ordered. "Otherwise the dining table might lose its colour."

He lifted the cover of a serving dish, "Mattar-panneer?"

"Don't you like mattar-panneer?"

"You must try and learn some Chinese and Italian dishes, too. I want to ask Pete Kendall and his wife to dinner next month. We must buy a barbecue for the balcony and by then we will have bought drapes — curtains — and maybe a new dinner set." He took in her silk salwar kameez but all he said was, "You need to buy some Canadian clothes, Devika. Try a skirt and blouse — it might suit you."

She changed the subject. "Why Chinese or Italian food? When they come, I will make them Indian food."

"No, no. Peter Kendall doesn't like the smell of curry."

"He doesn't like that powder they sell at Loblaws. I'm sure he's never had proper curry."

"One would think the recipe for proper curry was written in the Vedas. No, Devika — no curry. Besides," he said, loosening his tie, "I'm tired of curry. Make something else."

"Achcha." She hated arguments. "When . . . when will they be coming?"

"We didn't fix a date yet."

Devika had set the table for dinner hours ago, using the plates Ratan had bought on sale at the IGA store, but now she realized she'd set three places instead of two; Ratan, immersed in the *Star*, did not notice. There should be more people here. It wasn't right to have all this food and just the two of them, and no people except those faceless nameless people in cars for miles and miles around. Six or seven relatives, a few college friends or — looking at the table — four. Even if they were only three, it would be an improvement. One relative, maybe a friend.

Just one friend.

She placed a generous scoop of rice on his plate, then on her own and then, still musing, on the third plate.

Ratan lowered the paper and looked at her.

"Who's that for?"

"For my friend. Asha," said Devika. "She's hungry, too." She ladled mattar-panneer and chicken curry on the third plate, and poured a third glass of water as well.

"I don't see any Asha," said Ratan.

"She's right here," said Devika.

And then she was. Asha, filling an empty chair, making the unfamiliar empty space go away. Not reformed and docile Asha, not the Asha transformed by marriage, or the Asha so proud to have a son, but the old Asha, sitting right here in Toronto, looking at Mr. Right-Can-Do-No-Wrong Ratan with cynical amusement.

Ratan stood up from the table, scratching his head.

"Have you lost your mind?" he said.

She sat still, looking down at her plate. Asha smiled.

He picked up the offending plate and took it into the kitchen. She heard it slam on the Formica counter. Then he strode past her into the bedroom and soon she heard a small grunt as he took off his shoes. He came back barefoot, a comfort she'd heard him call an "ethnic" habit.

And there was the plate again, in front of Asha.

He shrugged. "Stop being stubborn, Devika, there's no one here."

"Asha is here."

He shook his head. "Women," he said.

Asha said to Devika, "Watch him think he can ignore me till I go away."

They ate in wary silence, and the plate remained. After dinner,

Devika washed and dried the dishes and stood on the balcony.

"What are you doing?" he asked.

"I'm showing Asha the lights of the CN Tower," she said.

"Come to bed." Irritation in the command.

A blue aerogramme slipped away and she watched it flutter down the Don Valley.

On Sunday at Vandana Di's house Ratan expounded on hot stocks to the men, neat J & B scotch swirling in a glass in his hand like the tawny golden eye of a tiger. Devika was in the kitchen with his sisters, and he felt liberated. Devika's Asha had begun to really grate on him. A little pretence lent a new wife a certain enigmatic charm; in fact, pretence could be quite romantic. But to invent a whole person who inhabited their new apartment and had to be fed and clothed . . . surely his parents should have checked with someone — Devika's family, neighbours, friends — someone should have known about these . . . well, hallucinations. Should he indulge her or should he put a stop to it? Ratan had been pointedly silent to show her his displeasure, a technique his father had used to good effect on his mother, but it wasn't working on Devika.

"Asha wants to go for a walk," Devika said after serving breakfast for three on Saturday. And then, instead of going to the grocery store in the car with Ratan, she took the elevator and he watched from the bedroom window as her tiny lone figure left the building. She scurried rabbit-like to the Philippine convenience store on the corner, and he watched till she emerged, saw her run all the way home, dupatta streaming behind her, as though Ravan himself were in pursuit. By the time she reached the apartment, he was back on the couch and absorbed in his stock analysis sheets, a briefcase of very important papers open on the coffee table before him.

Asha liked different clothes, too. Last week, Devika showed

him slick American magazines full of disdainful sullen-faced white women and pointed out the cowboy jean jackets and high-heeled boots that Asha liked. At last she was interested in something Canadian, so Ratan took her to Fairview Mall to buy them, and she tried them on for Asha — "Asha and I are the same size." But when they returned home, she locked them away in Asha's closet in the little bedroom. That, at any rate, was proper. He approved; he wouldn't want strange men to see her dressed in those clothes. But she'd locked away the high-heeled black patent leather shoes and the lingerie, as well. She was wasting his money.

One evening, there was the unmistakable smell of cigarette smoke and all the windows were open.

"Were you smoking?" he asked.

"Oh, no," Devika replied. "Asha likes a cigarette sometimes, it must have been her."

Asha, it turned out, didn't like the cheaper Canadian cigarettes — she liked Benson and Hedges. Asha was not neat and careful, like Devika. Devika threaded her rings on her watch strap and clasped the watch to her bedside lamp at night as though she were in a hotel, while Asha left little stubs in ashtrays in the spare bedroom, where the twin-size bed was always immaculate as a convent girl's, a long-haired doll on the white counterpane. (Ooff! He too was beginning to think of Asha as though she were real.) If Devika wanted to smoke and blame an imaginary woman, he wasn't going to let her think it bothered him. Besides, he was doing well. Even Peter Kendall had been impressed when he'd brought in three new clients this month. Ratan hadn't mentioned the last one was a Jew.

Asha's tastes were getting more expensive. Cocoa and bokchoy and marmite and marinated artichoke hearts. And now, "Asha wants a camera," Devika had informed him last night.

Maybe the camera was the answer. A new toy. It would distract Devika from this Asha nonsense, and she could take pictures from

the balcony and send them to her parents. She was always com-
plaining how homesick she felt. Then, when Devika was normal
again, he could ask Peter Kendall and his wife to dinner.

He turned to his brothers-in-law. They were older, they must
be consulted about expensive things like cameras. "I plan to buy
a camera," he said. "What would you suggest?"

His brothers-in-law drew round in solemn solidarity. They
considered, eyes raised to the ceiling, hands deep in their pockets or
twirling mustaches. Judgements were pronounced with finality.

"Nikon, bhai. Best. Top of the line."

"Ricoh, bhai. Can't miss.

"Get a Canon, Baba. You can always sell it in India."

He wouldn't take any of their advice, of course. If he took one
brother- in-law's advice, the other two would be insulted. But
if he hadn't asked for advice they would all have been mortally
wounded for a month.

Yes. A camera would be just the right thing.

Vandana Di came out of the kitchen bringing the smell of rice
and warm lemons. Ratan felt himself tense in case Devika had
been talking about Asha. But naturally Vandana had been talking
to Devika about her brother, not about Devika.

"So, Baba, when are you going to be promoted?"

Ratan bought Devika an Olympus camera and a twenty-four-
exposure Kodak film, because they were on sale. When he brought
it home, he was careful to say, "This is for Asha. I'll show you how
to use it, and you can show her."

There wasn't much to explain about the camera, but he spent
an hour advising her on composition, and ASA numbers, and
light and the importance of keeping the camera safe. It was the
most he had ever spoken to her, and he could feel her listening
with appropriate respect, so he was eloquent. He needed her

admiration that day. An old client of the firm had called Peter Kendall and accused Ratan of bad judgement in managing his portfolio. Peter Kendall had called him into his office and said, "Mr. Berton doesn't like a Paki managing his money. He has nothing against you personally, you know. He would just prefer to be with someone else."

"I understand," said Ratan, making his voice cheerful, willing, professional.

He'd told himself it didn't matter, and after work he'd stopped at the Hong Kong Camera discount store on Spadina to buy the camera, but then suddenly he'd given in to the anger. Pure anger, making him fight the rush-hour traffic as though he were driving in Delhi again, looping in and out and honking all the way to Little India on Gerrard Street. There he'd eaten chaat with his fingers, like a desi-dihaat from a village, and drunk a brown bottle of warm Rosy Pelican beer, as though daring Peter Kendall to drive by and see him.

Devika hadn't said anything about his being late. Hadn't asked him any questions about his day. Hadn't even met him at the door. She was in Asha's room with the door closed, talking. Taking both sides of the conversation, her high-pitched Lata Mangeshkar voice alternating with a lower, sexier, huskier tone. And an occasional laugh (he had never heard Devika laugh), a knowing, Asha laugh.

"What were you laughing at?"

"Asha was saying how white-skinned people think they look clean all the time so they don't bathe. *Chi*, dirty people."

She was, however, enchanted by the camera. She took his picture immediately. Then another and another. He was flattered, posing for her on the new couch, at the smoked-glass dining table, on the balcony, with the CN Tower behind. She stopped only when he told her not to finish the roll because, after all, film is expensive.

But when they sat down at the table, there were three place

settings again. Devika's plate had the camera beside it, lens pointed straight at Ratan. And as he, with mystified conscientiousness, watched the Maple Leafs play ice hockey on his new TV in the living room, Devika brought halwa in three dessert plates. And later he dreamed he was late for a meeting with Mr. Kendall and woke, sweating and in need of a woman, and he reached for her . . . but she was gone.

Ratan swore under his breath and found himself in Asha's room, and there was Devika, curled up on the white counterpane, asleep under a shawl. He scooped her up at the waist as though gathering a wayward kitten, and she fought his strength, his embrace, his very touch until he had her on the king-size bed and showed her struggle is futile.

He left early the next morning without breakfast, so she would feel appropriately guilty, and he went to bed without sitting down to dinner. He heard her with Asha at the dining table, talking like a crazy person to the air.

Devika rose at five in the morning. Ratan liked her to make alloo parathas for breakfast and a sandwich for his lunch and it took time. But last night, Asha and she had stayed up late, talking as they had in school, and now Devika was sleepy.

Asha was again the girl she used to be in college, before she was transformed by marriage. She was *there*, sitting cross-legged on the twin bed, angered as she used to be by things Devika never questioned, and they'd spent most of the night arguing, discussing. Asha wanted things Devika had never wanted. Asha wanted to take driving lessons. Asha wanted to visit Niagara Falls. Asha wanted to take flying lessons at Brampton Airport, instead of going and visiting Vandana Di every Sunday. Asha wanted to climb the CN Tower and go to Canada's Wonderland *all alone*. Asha wanted to know how it felt to ride a horse bareback. Asha thought love should make a woman feel like a banana split with all three scoops melting inside. Asha wanted to ride a fork-lift truck and wear a hard hat and overalls. Asha wanted to drive all the way to Vancouver with a CB radio and a trucker who could sing woeful country ballads. Asha wanted to talk and have someone listen, someone besides Devika. That strong will, that unfettered enthusiasm for every experience, that appetite. That unadulterated, unmasked, *selfishness*. Haw, ji, haw . . . Shame! Devika had tried to reason with her all night.

"Asha," she'd said. "You should be grateful. You have a loving family. You have parents who trusted you enough to send you abroad *alone* to visit me. You have good looks. You have a wealthy husband to take care of you. You even have a son. What more can a woman ask for?"

"Love," said Asha.

"You have love," said Devika wretchedly. "You have family who take care of you."

"Taking care of me is not Love," said Asha, deep-voiced as the low string on a sitar. "I have people who love me because I am there. Not people who love me because they know me."

"But Asha, you are so difficult to love. I'm sure everyone would love you if you would only be nice. Is that so difficult? To just be nice?"

And Asha had responded as though they had still been melodramatic little children in pigtails wearing candy-striped frocks to school. She had risen from the little bed and thrown the trusting, wondering, innocent, long-haired doll out of the window. Twenty-one stories.

Devika had recoiled in fright.

She decided Asha needed to worship more. Worship keeps you from thinking about why things are the way they are and even about why things are not the way they could be. She stood on a stepladder in the kitchen and lifted the black metal statue of dancing

Lord Shiva out of obscurity in the cabinet over the refrigerator where Ratan had banished him. Contemplation of the Nataraj with his powerful foot on the neck of ignorance would bring Asha a better sense of her own insignificance. Devika carried the idol to Asha's room, set it on the bed where the long-haired doll had lain and closed the door behind her.

Because surely that was the real problem. Asha had become a woman who had made the mistake of believing she was somehow . . . *significant.*

All the pictures on the first roll of film were of Ratan, and his sisters approved. Devika gave them the ones they wanted and set about hunting Ratan again, so she could take his picture unawares. He began to feel as though she were stalking him as a panther stalks a kakar in the terrai. He took two rolls in for developing and found not a single picture of the apartment, not one picture taken from the balcony. Not one picture of maple leaves turning red and gold in the Don Valley, or the CN Tower against a sunset. All pictures of Ratan, as though she wanted to have him, a piece of him, all the time. And they weren't even nice pictures; his hair was thinning.

In fact, his hair was falling out in patches. There were small bald spots on the back of his head, and he took himself to the emergency room at North York Hospital.

"Stress-related," said the doctor from Poland. But for Ratan, there was a jeer in his voice, the older immigrant's snigger. *Sissy, it was ten times more difficult when I came here. You just can't take it. What will you do if you don't have what it takes, can't make it?* "But," continued the doctor, "nothing to worry about."

He thought of telling the doctor his stress was all Devika's fault. Devika and her Asha friend . . . *imaginary* friend. No, he couldn't tell the doctor that, couldn't bother the doctor with women's problems. And Canada was causing his stress, and so was Peter Kendall, with his return-on-investment figures and his graphs and his market statistics. The rules are simple enough: low risk, low reward; high risk, high reward. The immigrant mantra. Still, Peter Kendall pored over his LOTUS 1-2-3 spreadsheets with their what-if analyses that couldn't beat a Turk reading tea leaves.

And so were his family causing this stress. Letters from his parents telling him to find a Canadian company interested in a joint venture and come home with dollars in his pockets. Vandana Di's remarks about loving sisters and their husbands who helped their only brother come to Canada so the whole family could do well. And Devika was not helping at all. Ratan was beginning to feel she was daring him every day. Daring him to prove he could make her happy, to prove that giving up her family and coming to Canada was worth it. Daring him to take Asha and make her disappear.

He had to drive her to Loblaws, write the cheque, manage everything. She couldn't even remember his PIN number for the cash machine. She was helpless before the simple task of cleaning the bathtub. How had she ever graduated from college? Maybe her parents had lied to his about that.

She couldn't even remember to press B for Basement, so they always had to stop in the lobby and look foolish as people tried to join them on the elevator. "Going down. Going down," he would tell them, letting the closing door obliterate the mocking vanilla faces.

He tried to teach Devika to drive, but either she was too nervous or he was too impatient. She would not remember to fasten her lap-belt even though he'd told her the police could charge him a fifty-dollar fine for her stupidity. And the simple sequence "mirror — signal — shoulder check" was enough to reduce her to tears. Vandana Di said he should get her a few driving lessons, but why should he pay for some strange man to teach her what he knew already? Besides, there was a certain power in telling her what to do and having her fail; it made him feel, well . . . larger.

"Asha says her ears hurt when you shout," said Devika, letting Her Invisible Highness out of the back seat after one such lesson.

"Tell Asha her ears are really going to hurt when I catch them and twist them off her nasty little head," said Ratan. The threat felt good. In fact, it needed embellishing. "Tell Asha she can go back to India because I'm ready to wring her ugly little neck."

And Devika stood there with that look of fragile innocence betrayed till he relented and said, "All right. Tell Asha she can stay." Then, with a flash of inspiration, he added, "For another week."

But at the end of the week, Asha was "very sick with a backache" and could not be moved.

"I'll go in and talk with her, I'll find out how she is," said Ratan.

He knocked with an elaborate flourish at the door to the spare room. The Nataraj Shiva lay like a black spider on the counterpane and the room was still. Devika watched him from the living room.

"Asha wants a massage," said Ratan, and closed the door.

He sat in the little room for a long, long while, looking at the open closet with the high-heeled cowboy boots, the black patent leather shoes, the jean jacket, the motorcycle helmet, the bikini underwear, the printed socks, the lace camisole, the red velvet swing coat, the lipsticks and the rhinestone tiara and all the other trinkets she had made him buy . . . for Asha. And he wished Asha were a real person who would love him, Ratan.

But she wasn't.

So he went back to Devika, saying, "Give her an aspirin."

Devika, memorizer of TV commercials, said, "Tylenol is better."

Why, if she were pretending, couldn't she also pretend to be jealous? Every picture she took was of Ratan, every minute of her day was spent in cooking, cleaning and waiting for him. She listened every time he had something to tell her. Everyone knows love isn't what's shown in the movies, but all the same, it's just *courteous* to be jealous if your husband suggests giving another woman, even an imaginary one, a massage.

Peter Kendall said the snow had come early. He'd said that last year and probably would say it every year with that same look of glad surprise. Ratan, however, wasn't quite as thrilled. Slippery-grey slush pocked Highway 401 for the weekly visits to Brampton, Malton or Mississauga, and he wasn't very good at steering in the direction of the car's slide. And Toronto was grey, grey, grey as Peter Kendall's Establishment hair. While his was black and falling. He was leaving pieces of himself everywhere, all over Toronto, and what parts of him were left were being taken from him slowly, surreptitiously, with Devika's damnable pictures, the flash going off from crazy angles into his sleep-dazed or blinking eyes.

It had to stop.

"Asha thinks you should get a life insurance policy," Devika said on Sunday morning.

"And what do *you* think?"

"I?" She was caught unawares. It was a question he had never asked before.

"Yes, you. I don't see anyone else here."

"Asha . . ." she began.

"No. Not Asha. You. What do *you* think? You think I should buy a life insurance policy?"

"As you wish," said Devika.

Why could the women in his life not tell him things, tell him what they wanted, instead of hinting to him, poking at him with their sly insinuations, their arch expectations, their snide challenging, their sultry little silences and their sweet little games, as though he were a cobra with drained poison sacs and they the snake-charmers pretending to fear, pretending to worship, pretending, pretending. Women's shakti is dangerous unless harnessed or wounded.

"Chalo," he said. "Vandana Di will be waiting."

"Asha is ready."

She looked so convent-girl *Indian*, constantly adjusting that impractical marigold-yellow silk dupatta, that he wanted to shake her. She'd forget her coat as usual; he wouldn't remind her. Let the Canadian winter teach her the lesson it had taught him; next time she'd remember her coat.

"Are *you* ready?"

"Mmmhmm." Again that surprise.

They were picking up speed on the ramp to the 401 when she looked at her lap in dismay.

"Just a minute. My dupatta is caught in the door."

Before he could stop her, she had pulled at the handle. The Tempo door flew open and there was a whirr as the automatic shoulder strap released her. The car slithered over an ice patch and veered away from her flying body. He saw the unused lap belt glisten in the corner of his eye as he tried to brake, tried to call, tried to stop her going away from him.

When he reached her, she had struggled to her knees, one hand covering her naked throat. And she was crawling, sobbing, dishevelled, towards the sodden shreds of her dupatta. She was almost to it, scrabbling in the muck like a madwoman for any passing Canadian to see, and he heard himself snarl, "See what happens when you don't listen to me."

That stopped her, stopped her crawling and that awful, vulnerable whimper, and she lay quiet, shocked, along the melting snowbank.

For the first time, she suffered him to touch her in daylight. So he held her, small and shivering in the cold grey foreignness, until the ambulance came.

A vase of plastic flowers stood, determinedly cheerful, on the night-stand. A woman doctor's voice. "Some concussion, bruises and a broken arm. You're very lucky you weren't killed, but we'll have to watch you over the next few weeks."

An earnest white policeman with a cold took her statement.

"You say you opened the door — "

"My dupatta was caught in the door," she explained.

The policeman sneezed. He wrote, "Scarf . . . caught . . . in . . . passenger . . . door."

She pointed to his pad with an effort.

"Not my scarf, my dupatta."

"How do you spell that?" The policeman wiped his nose.

"D-U-P-A-T-T-A," she intoned.

A dupatta is more, so much more than a scarf. It is a woman's modesty, her goodness, to be protected, cherished by her husband. She wanted her mother, her father, and at least twenty solicitous relatives telling her what to do, how to do it, how to live, how to be good, how to be loved.

But here there was only Ratan, *Canadian* Ratan, sitting in the sterile whiteness watching the green glow of digital displays on the monitor and the slow weave of the plotter recording her brain wave patterns from the greased electrodes at her temples.

There was only Ratan, and Canada, and herself. No one else.

Ratan loomed over her.

"How are you, Devika?" he asked.

She tried to smile then, but the bruises on her face were too painful. She felt him sit next to her on the bed and winced as he took her hand. How was she?

"I am Asha," she said, voice low and husky. "Devika was afraid of living here, so she just . . . flew away."

Ratan came closer. Asha, Devika — all the same to him. "Asha," he said, as though testing the name. The name means hope.

"When you look better, Asha," he told her, "I will invite Peter Kendall and his wife to dinner."

"When I feel better," said Asha, "I want . . ." Speaking was difficult. "I want . . . to go to Niagara Falls." And because Asha could live even if Ratan were to die, she said, "I want to take pictures of the falls and send them home to India."

Then Asha closed her swollen eyes and felt Devika drift away as though she had never been.

Afterword

Apprehending the Shape of Experience — Shauna Singh Baldwin's Stories

by KULDIP GILL

Opening the pages of Shauna Singh Baldwin's *English Lessons and Other Stories* is like taking a pilgrimage, a journey, or even a walking tour. Along the way, one encounters many contexts where one lingers or revisits and experiences the plight of many characters, each more interesting than the last.

The first time I sat down to read this collection, I could not start the second story until I had read "Rawalpindi, 1919" at least three times. It moved me in a very personal way — something I had not previously felt with any other story. I asked myself, "Why?" and I found that Shauna Singh Baldwin had captured my attention through details and imagery.

In the story she describes how an Indian woman makes chapatti dough, which acts as a symbol that sheds light upon the narrative. To follow the story, we must pay attention to the chappati dough. I know how it feels to make the dough — know how once I've finished kneading it, I too form a ball of it and turn its rough side down, patting the top to make it shine. I've also taken a small piece out and gone through the steps the author describes. If the phone rings or something else interrupts the process, the small piece, exposed to air, will quickly begin to develop a looser structure and a different colour, taking on a different complexion from the main body of dough.

As I read, my hands could feel the dough and itched to move as Baldwin gave the details of the process. She wants the reader to experience the act of making dough, and so uses all her artistry as a writer.

The dough is a metaphor for life, family, and universal values. For the metaphor to convey the meanings intended, we must be attentive to cultural nuances. In this story, Baldwin includes compelling scenes that portray collectivist cultural values. Separated from his family, the boy Sarup will take on the individualist values of the West. His mother knows that if they refuse to let their son go to England, he may remain more true to family values.

Despite this intuitive knowledge, the mother knows she must be prepared to let him go, but will not do so without making her husband, who wants the son to be educated in England, aware of what they can anticipate on their son's return. She takes food to her husband in the manner of an Indian wife. As she observes the family values of service to a husband, she talks to him in culturally specific ways. She suggests to him that if the boy goes away to an English school, he will return with foreign tastes and different needs and desires. There is a hint of threat that the husband had better be prepared. In fact, they had better buy some china dinnerware (the old metal thali won't do). When their son returns, he will not be content with pillows on the floor — a sofa had better be in the plans, as well.

Through this first story we also learn of and adjust to the evocative language used and familiarize ourselves with Baldwin's style and the riches of the Punjabi language.

Baldwin uses words, images, and concepts from different languages or dialects throughout her work, and different registers within these languages. I was constantly surprised at how easy she made it appear to show the thoughts of particular individuals as well as the dialogue between them. This seeming effortlessness exists despite the breadth: stories are told about different classes of people, in diverse voices. We hear the voices of an old woman, a young girl, a young married woman, and the voice of a woman about to be engaged. The ease belies a well-honed writing style — how else could she tell of ground-level relationships, with characters emerging through confessional modes of thought? She knows each character's inner language at an intimate level and allows us to enter it. Familiar with these languages and cultures, I found the range of stories immensely credible and satisfying to read, in all their complexity.

I can't help but notice the details in these stories. One insightful passage from "Family Ties" illustrates Baldwin's expertise in presenting important particulars. The story opens in the voice of the narrator — a ten-year-old girl who is "absurdly happy" with her father's attention to her as his beti (daughter). He calls her by a pet name, his little "kukri" (a small hen) because she is a fearful little thing. She tells us later that she is entrusted to go to the market with their driver, and to the chicken-seller to buy the meat for dinner.

> The hens all look the same to me — brownish-white
> with frightened eyes, silly kukris just like me. I look
> at the closest cage and one steps forward. She holds
> her head high when she crows, thrusts her breast at
> the cage and seems unafraid to die, so I say, "That
> one." A moment later her head is severed and Nand
> Singh throws her in his shopping bag. Although
> Mummy's frown at my plate warns that no one will
> marry a fatty, I eat the curried kukri that night,
> hoping her courage will nourish mine.

*

As I read, I attend to details such as pet names and words, for this is how Baldwin foreshadows the unfolding plot. These rich elements provide us with the life of the family sequentially through the teenage years of our young narrator, who tells us of the lessons she accumulates: "But I have learned, learned that to be part of a family you have to agree to keep its secrets. Because there are penalties to be paid by kukris who crow." She has imbibed what Baldwin shows us in other stories throughout this collection: that traditionally, women had to learn silence, for women who didn't comply with traditional modes of living were severely punished.

I felt that each of the women protagonists in Baldwin's stories, though sometimes simple, showed that every person has unique, even extraordinary qualities. Human nature and dignity are qualities we must value and respect; they inspire a "bottomless well of empathy and compassion" for all of mankind.

Shauna Singh Baldwin has a good measure of compassion for the characters, especially the women she depicts in her complex and multi-layered stories; a lesson in good literature. A story that best demonstrates this is "A Pair of Ears," where Baldwin shows insight into human nature. She shows us the compassion, empathy, and love a housekeeper (Amma) has for her dead mistress who was treated badly by her greedy son and daughter-in-law. Amma says, "I squat again. I paint slowly — for this is important — slowly I paint a rangoli design in my Mem-saab's blood on the white chip marble floor." Baldwin can empathize with the maidservant's desire to leave a vengeful symbol for them — a symbol in the blood of a woman whose son put her through agony.

In a recent essay on Dostoevsky published in *Brick* magazine, Orhan Pamuk writes, "he refused to offer up his wisdom in the abstract, instead he locates these truths inside characters that give every impression of being real." Similarly, in this collection of short stories, time and again, Baldwin gives us characters we believe in, who live on in our minds.

She reveals the complicated textures of the lives of South Asian women in all of their absurdities and painful truths through these tales. Her particular style of writing, humorous at times, is also full of fresh similes and metaphors that can only come from a writer knowledgeable in a number of languages — their peculiar idioms and puns. Again and again I enjoyed her use of literature's many conventions, such as figurative language. In "Gayatri," she opens the story with the protagonist "cocooned in a sulk." Then she tells us that the "heat of a new Delhi morning panted like a waiting dog." Suddenly, we feel the bodily discomfort caused by an oppressively hot day in India.

Baldwin is adept at entering the minds of her characters to show us the different ways her protagonists think about traditional and ethical values, and the way they act on their own choices. I found that she uses the conventions of writing to advantage. In "The Insult," she uses a family gathering to demonstrate how two sisters interact. Aunty Nimmi's denial of help to find a mate in India for her niece, and the subsequent alienation of the two sisters is shown through dialogue. As readers, we can see characters develop through a particular scene in which the narrator says, "My mother sighed. She had asked a favour, and she had been refused." They engage in some other dialogue for a few minutes, and when the sister persists and hints for help again: "Aunty Nimmi laughed. 'There are many nice Sikh boys in Chicago.' Again she had missed her cue."

These kinds of scenes in Baldwin's work resonate deeply with my experiences in South Asian culture, and I'm delighted with her portrayals. I have used only a few of the fifteen stories that illustrate this throughout the collection. The author is an adept, artistic stylist who divulges the quotidian and the everyday home scene, first-person narrative, reflective personal interior monologues of her characters, third-person narrative, and other strategies which surface with careful reading, showing a sweet compassion and empathy for the lives of the human beings who populate her stories; I will remember them.

References

Orhan Pamuk, "On Dostoevsky." *Brick, A Literary Journal*. Issue 80, Winter 2007.

Reader's Guide

About the Author

To celebrate the lasting potency and relevance of *English Lessons and Other Stories*, Goose Lane Editions presents the *Reader's Guide Edition* of Shauna Singh Baldwin's first short story collection. Since this remarkable literary debut, her work has been translated into thirteen languages.

From her beginnings as a radio producer and ecommerce consultant, Baldwin's writing career took off with *English Lessons and Other Stories* in 1996, winning the Friends of American Writers Award. Since then, she has published two novels with Knopf Canada: the best-selling *What the Body Remembers*, which won the Commonwealth Writer's Prize (Canada and Caribbean), and *The Tiger Claw*, finalist for the Giller Prize. Her impact on the international literary scene is undeniable.

Shauna returned to Goose Lane Editions in 2007 with another short story collection, *We Are Not in Pakistan*. Her work continues to garner praise from a worldwide readership. Her fiction, poems, and essays have been published in a broad spectrum of literary and popular magazines, anthologies, and newspapers.

Born in Montreal, Shauna Singh Baldwin grew up in India. She lives in Milwaukee, Wisconsin, with her Irish-American husband, David.

An Interview with the Author

GLE: The stories in *English Lessons and Other Stories* often revolve around clashes of culture and values within families, as family members struggle to adapt to life in North America. What were your greatest challenges in bringing this dynamic to light through these characters?

SSB: I'd say my greatest challenge was portraying multilingual characters in one language. Like any language, English has limitations. It's heavily weighted with Biblical references and colonial connotations, so it's less user-friendly for descriptions of non-European settings and people. On the plus side, compared to gendered languages that reinforce assumptions about gender in every interaction — Hindi, Punjabi, Urdu, and many European languages like Spanish and French — it may be somewhat less loaded for writing about women.

Because English is the most powerful global language, learning it brings a cultural shift, often of power. As the mother in "Rawalpindi 1919" realizes, learning English or going abroad changes relationships for the person who leaves and for family members who stay.

GLE: You tell tales in the first and third person. How do you decide which to use when you're telling a story?

SSB: I let a story and its characters tell me if it should be told in first or third person, experimenting till the narrative distance feels natural. "Rawalpindi 1919," "English Lessons," and "Toronto 1984" use interior monologue as if someone were writing in a diary — naturally, in first person. "Family Ties" is in first person, but it feels to me as if Fatty is reliving her story under hypnosis. The third person, in stories like "Gayatri," "A Pair of Ears," "Nothing Must Spoil This Visit," and "Devika," introduces a narrator. Sometimes that's necessary for distance, commentary, or explanation. I feel my way by character and length, considering the reader in due course.

GLE: Two of your characters provide us with the point of view of white women married to or in relationships with Sikh men: Janet in "Nothing Must Spoil This Visit" and Lisa in "Lisa." What did these points of view bring to this collection of stories?

SSB: Unlike Jassie who speaks of "white women" as she tells her story, I prefer the term women of European origin. Janet is married to Arvind in "Nothing Must Spoil This Visit," and Arvind is a Sikh. But the unnamed man who is going with Lisa might be Sikh, Hindu, Jain, Buddhist, or Muslim — the religion is left to the reader. Without these tales in the collection you'd only read stories about people of Indian origin adapting to the West. But I feel people of European origin need to adapt, too.

Intercultural relationships frequently involve the discovery of differing values: individual rights versus family honour in "Nothing Must Spoil This Visit" or romantic love versus son-preference in "Lisa." Janet is a well-meaning romantic whose blithe assumptions are challenged by the idea that her happiness is founded on Chaya's unhappiness — and she doesn't know the whole story. Lisa isn't interested in understanding cultural differences, so she'll make the same mistake again.

GLE: In "A Pair of Ears," Balvir's blind greed and heartless treatment of his mother, though treated within the context of Indian society, transcends cultural barriers. How is the absence of the theme of clashing cultures in this story important to this collection?

SSB: Elder abuse happens in every culture, but stands out in one that prides itself on highly valuing and respecting its elders. Also, as I learned in writing this story, Amma, a Hindu serving woman who owns almost nothing, paradoxically has richer relationships of sharing with her children and more freedom than her mem-saab, the upper-class/upper-caste Sikh woman. I included it because it shows the impact of Western values and standards about youth and the imperative of progress. Here I'm thinking of Balvir's projected condominium complex! These are English lessons too, learned from three hundred years of contact with and colonization by the British.

GLE: Both Indian and Western culture have naming traditions that illustrate male ownership of women. In Western culture, a woman takes her husband's last name. In Indian culture, the husband chooses a new first name for his wife. Do you see a similarity between these naming conventions?

SSB: As alluded to in "Jassie," Indian husbands often chose new first names for their wives up to the 1940s. It's rare in urban post-independence India. Today, like women in the West, urban Indian women have begun to keep their birth family names for career reasons.

And yes, such naming conventions betray similar cultural

assumptions. They assume women and women's wombs are family property, and that the male line carries the family name and assets. As in Europe, the custom of primogeniture was re-enforced by the British in India for efficiency of taxation.

GLE: This story collection begins in 1919 and continues chronologically until the present day. Was the arrangement meaningful? I wanted more stories past 1991!

SSB: I wanted to explore the changes for Indian women in my three countries (India, Canada, and the US) over the years. I began after the First World War and the influenza epidemic in India, when learning English and becoming like the British was an end in itself. I found stark contrasts between the values of urban Indians within India and the Diaspora versus the West and the situation of Indian women versus the West. In 1991, problems and opportunities for Indian women shifted, when the Indian economy opened to the import of Western goods. Technology shifted, Indian men and women vaulted into the era of TVs with remotes, then fax machines, then computers and cellphones. English remains the ticket to the global economy, but different problems emerge after 1991.

GLE: Maybe that's a future book. Can you talk about the difference between this collection of stories and your latest, *We Are Not in Pakistan*, published eleven years later?

SSB: The stories in *English Lessons and Other Stories* deal with Indian men and women. The stories in *We Are Not in Pakistan* take place in the late '90s and post 9/11 world and only some have Indian characters. They are set in the Ukraine, the US, Canada, and Costa Rica. Some are from the point of view of women, some from the point of view of men — one is from the point of view of a

Lhasa Apso! The characters are negotiating the issues of our times —
nuclear power, our ambivalent relationship with Art, issues of race,
class, gender, human, and civil rights.

GLE: There was a long hiatus between your two short story col-
lections, during which you wrote two novels. What impelled you
to the stories in the second collection?

SSB: After writing about the 1947 Partition of India in *What the
Body Remembers* and Europe during the Second World War in
The Tiger Claw, I wanted a break from war and history and the
sad treatment of women in both. But these subjects refuse to go
away — the "war on terror" is underpinned by cultural assumptions about whether the economic well-being of the developed
nations must rest on the economic exploitation of people and re-
sources in the developing world. And cultural assumptions about
whether women are people, what women want or need, and
whether a woman owns her own body. I began by writing one
story but soon heard more voices, each demanding I tell his or her
story. I needed to explore contemporary issues again, with echoes
of the history I'd learned from writing the novels. Before I knew
it, I had committed another book: *We Are Not in Pakistan*.

Books of Interest
Selected by the Author

When I began writing *English Lessons and Other Stories* in 1991, I was producer and host of a radio show called *Sunno!, the East Indian American radio show where you don't have to be East Indian to listen.* I wanted to air stories in English about Indian women (and men) but soon realized I would have to write the kind of stories I wanted. Other writers who have felt a similar need:

Incantations and Other Stories by Anjana Appachana
Junglee Girl by Ginu Kamani
Arranged Marriage: Stories by Chitra Divakaruni
Interpreter of Maladies by Jhumpa Lahiri

Few books trace the women's movement in India both legally and in cultural practice. Here's one I would love to see updated for this decade:

The History of Doing: An Illustrated History of Movements for Women's Rights and Feminism in India by Radha Kumar.

The stories in *English Lessons* feature Hindu and Sikh women. Hinduism is commonly understood, so here are a few books on Sikhism:

> *Sikhism: A Very Short Introduction* by Eleanor Nesbitt
> *The Sikhs: Their Religious Beliefs and Practices* by William
>   Owen Cole and Piara Singh Sambhi
> *Ethics of the Sikhs* by Avtar Singh — I would have titled this
>   book "The Religious Philosophy of Sikhism." It's an excellent introduction to the teachings of the ten Gurus.

I discover more facets each time I read these works of fiction:

Hard Times by Charles Dickens
Horses are a motif in the interior décor of our home, including the wallpaper. One of my favourite scenes in *Hard Times* is when a gentleman discusses wallpapering a room.

> "I'll explain to you then," said the gentleman after a
> dismal pause, "why you wouldn't paper a room with
> representations of horses. Do you ever see horses
> walking up and down the sides of rooms in reality —
> in fact? Do you?" . . . "Why then you are not to see
> any where, what you don't see in fact; you are not to
> have anywhere, what you don't have in fact. What is
> called taste is only another name for fact."

If you are writing fiction, this gentleman lies in wait for you, if not in real life then in your mind.

Alice in Wonderland by Lewis Caroll
Alice remains calm, sensible, reasonable, caring and helpful when the world around her turns topsy-turvy, and as she and people around her make silly statements, change in unpredictable ways, vanish, and create problems. I know quite a few women like her.

Nectar in a Sieve by Kamala Markandaya
Few writers can write "down class" without romanticising or con-
descending. Kamala Markandaya is pitch-perfect. Reading her work
widens your compassion and intelligence.

The Handmaid's Tale by Margaret Atwood
When I read the story of surrogate mother Offred I knew so little
about writing I wondered if Atwood's experiences were anything
like the women she described. How else did she know about the
misogyny so many women consider normal? It was one of the few
novels that discussed the power relationships between women,
circumstances of surrogate motherhood, and polygamy, a topic I
explored more than a decade later when writing *What the Body
Remembers*.

Days of the Turban by Pratap Sharma
My favourite of all Pratap Sharma's plays, novels, and films.
Days of the Turban tells the story of Balbir from Amritsar who
becomes involved with protesters who become revolutionaries,
then extremists, and finally terrorists. It's written with great love,
understanding, and sorrow for families in Punjab who lost so many
sons in the eighties.

Come Rain by Jai Nimbkar
A wonderfully nuanced look at cultural conflicts. Ann Palmer
meets a middle-class foreign student, Ravi Gogte, in San Francisco
and moves to India to live with him and his family. Ann doesn't
have blonde hair, is not promiscuous, nor bothered by India's dirt
and squalor. She isn't even a missionary. Ann has a stormy relationship with her husband and a number of power struggles with
a very strong mother-in-law. Her efforts to understand India are
skilfully rendered by Nimbkar's smooth and thoughtful dialogue.

A book that flows as well as this one could not have been easy to write.

Fugitive Pieces by Anne Michaels
My husband David was away on a business trip, and I planned to finish *Fugitive Pieces,* the story of Jakob Beer, a Polish Jewish boy who witnesses the slaughter of his family in the Holocaust. When I couldn't find the novel anywhere, I called David to ask if he had seen it. "I hid it," he said without a trace of shame, "because it made you cry so much." "I cried because it was so touching and beautiful," I said. On his return, I demanded my book, but David (genuinely!) couldn't remember where he'd put it. "It will show up eventually," he said. I couldn't wait for eventually. I was scheduled to speak at BookExpo Canada on a panel with Anne Michaels. I bought a US edition of the book so I could ask Anne to sign it. Now we own two copies, and both are precious.

The Telling by Ursula Le Guin
Reading *A Wizard of Earthsea* as a child, I wondered what Ursula Le Guin would be like in person. I'm still wondering, because she chooses the style and voice that suits each story. I now know how difficult that is. She's an anthropologist, feminist, and an explorer of the impact of technology. *The Telling* is one of my favourites: the story of emissary Sutty, who moves to the north of the planet Aka to find people unaffected by the rule of the Dovzan Corporation, "inefficient people" whose way of learning is through ideograms and story. Her journey is monitored by the Corporation but equally interesting is how she monitors herself as an observer who must make a report without HP (hocus-pocus). If you're a writer, read *A Wave in the Mind* as well.

Plowing the Dark by Richard Powers
In the early days of virtual reality, the long-ago eighties, a team of programmers realize an artist is required to make a virtual world. Enter Adie from New York, a character who gives rise to the most amazing descriptions of computer art you've ever read. Alongside, Powers describes the virtual world of memory created by an English teacher from Chicago captured by terrorists in Beirut, Lebanon. The twined stories in this brilliant novel link memory and the future. Powers captures the wonder and delight of creating a virtual world in story, without shying from the political implications of technology.

Slow Emergencies by Nancy Huston
Lin Lhomond has two beautiful girls whom she loves, yet she chooses ballet over being a mother and a wife, and her choice affects the whole family. Nancy Huston's words are so well chosen they are transparent, allowing her story to shine through. It's also poetry without line breaks. Whether you have children or not, have faced the woman artist's dilemma or not, you'll recognize the ever-present distance between real-life obligations joyfully assumed and the life you'd like to lead. And — what if?

Changing Planes by Ursula K. Le Guin
Stories that take off from an airport terminal waiting area — except that you visit different planets and societies. Le Guin offers new perspectives, plays what-if scenarios, teases your brain, and makes you feel strongly about people not of your species.

The Time of Our Singing by Richard Powers
A German physicist meets a black singer at the Marian Anderson concert in Washington DC in 1941; they fall in love, marry, and have three children. Their mixed-race family's saga is told mostly by their second son looking back from 2000, recounting

with understated pathos how he was always pulled between his older brother and sister. Histories of racism and Western music come entwined in this sweeping complex novel of 600 plus pages. Every sentence is so beautifully crafted; I was not surprised to learn Powers was a programmer in the days when disk space and processor time came at a premium.

The Hungry Tide by Amitav Ghosh
Delhi-based entrepreneur Kanai Dutt meets marine biologist Piyali (Piya) Roy in the tide country of the Sunderbans. Piya is a second-generation Indo-American marine biologist studying the ways of the Irrawady Dolphin. By the end of the novel, events force Kania and Piya to do without texts or data and reinterpret their time in the tide country. Each must make a greater effort to communicate between English and non-English speakers, oral and written traditions, and across class and religious divides. Amitav Ghosh is in full command as he tells this prophetic and disturbing tale. Every chapter develops slowly as a wave, then ebbs, leaving a nugget that compels you further into this powerful, moving novel. I did wonder why Piya never menstruates, never thinks about having/not having children, is unaware of having breasts or uterus, and never exhibits sexual desire. But at least here's a woman who loves her work and believes in understanding rather than hunting animals. Offering old "Mashima" — NGO founder, quiet builder of a hospital — Ghosh pays tribute to legions of dedicated women whose social work has crossed class boundaries throughout South-East Asia and supported women in changing their own lives.

Can You Hear the Nightbird Call? by Anita Rau Badami
A novel with heart, history, finesse, and some hugely funny moments. It brought me to tears several times. It is true to the time of its tale, and describes us halfway-house Indo-Canadians so

well, the characters are still with me. I stayed up till 1:00 a.m. to finish it, and couldn't get to sleep for hours afterwards because the ending is so harrowing. Read slowly to really savour this superb novel and just don't let it end.

Song of Kahunsha by Anosh Irani

This is the tale of an orphan boy in Bombay. Comparisons to *Oliver Twist* are spurious — this novel is in a class by itself. Human Rights Watch says, "At least eighteen million children live or work on the streets of urban India, labouring as porters at bus or railway terminals; as mechanics in informal auto-repair shops; as vendors of food, tea, or handmade articles; as street tailors; or as rag pickers, picking through garbage and selling usable materials to local buyers." Irani's simple, unassuming prose asks us to feel deeply for just three of them: Chamdi, Sumdi, and Guddi dream of a city of no sadness called Kahunsha. I will never stand at the Gateway of India in Bombay without remembering Guddi, that little girl singing her "Song of Kahunsha."

Orpheus Lost by Janette Turner Hospital

This book deals with our strange civil rights situations post 9/11, terrorism, and rendition, all through the Orpheus myth. The predicament of Leela the mathematician from South Carolina and her lover Mishka, a half-Muslim Australian musician kept me awake at night. I kept reminding myself that Cobb, the interrogator who goes too far is "just" a character and that *Orpheus Lost* is "just" a novel. A devilishly smart and prescient novel by a mistress of the art.

Echomaker by Richard Powers

Mark Schluter, victim of a truck accident, is afflicted with a brain condition called capgras, so he can no longer recognize his sister Karen. Along comes Gerald Weber, celebrity neuroscientist, whose created persona seems to be unravelling as he questions all that he knows about the brain. Powers shows the beauty and flaws of modern neuroscience in this complex and personal novel. What do we really know of the three-and-a-half-pound universe we're carrying around, or the self it creates? Maybe the vedas are right after all — it's all maya, all illusion. I also enjoyed the audio edition, unobtrusively narrated by Bernadette Dunn.-